"I didn't mean to pry."

"You're fine. It's just…" Daria released a breath. "My sister and I were raised in the system." Tyler's confusion must have shown because she added, "Foster kids."

"Oh. Wow. That must have been rough."

"Could've been worse." She paused at a T in the trail. "Heading west, it continues through more of what we've just walked through. It thins out some going eastward." She pointed that direction. "Through a small slice of county-owned land before cutting through your family's property."

In other words, she wanted to change the subject. He understood that. As if losing her sister hadn't been painful enough, the poor woman had obviously endured a great deal in her life. Hardship that could've turned her bitter or motivated her to give up entirely.

And yet here she was, fighting to give her niece and nephew the best life possible.

His admiration for her grew whenever they interacted. If he wasn't careful, when the time came for him to leave, his heart would be in a heap of trouble.

Jennifer Slattery is a writer and speaker who has addressed women's and church groups across the nation. As the founder of Wholly Loved Ministries, she and her team help women rest in their true worth and live with maximum impact. When not writing, Jennifer loves spending time with her adult daughter and hilarious husband. Visit her online at jenniferslatterylivesoutloud.com to learn more or to book her for your next women's event.

Books by Jennifer Slattery

Love Inspired

Restoring Her Faith
Hometown Healing
Building a Family
Chasing Her Dream
Her Small-Town Refuge
Falling for the Family Next Door

Visit the Author Profile page at LoveInspired.com for more titles.

Falling for the Family Next Door

Jennifer Slattery

LOVE INSPIRED

INSPIRATIONAL ROMANCE

LOVE INSPIRED®

INSPIRATIONAL ROMANCE

Recycling programs
for this product may
not exist in your area.

ISBN-13: 978-1-335-59682-6

Falling for the Family Next Door

Copyright © 2023 by Jennifer Slattery

For questions and comments about the quality of this book, please contact us
at CustomerService@Harlequin.com.

Love Inspired
22 Adelaide St. West, 41st Floor
Toronto, Ontario M5H 4E3, Canada
www.LoveInspired.com

Printed in U.S.A.

Blessed be God, even the Father of our Lord Jesus Christ, the Father of mercies, and the God of all comfort; Who comforteth us in all our tribulation, that we may be able to comfort them which are in any trouble, by the comfort wherewith we ourselves are comforted of God.

—2 Corinthians 1:3–4

To my daughter and son-in-law,
Ashley and Angel Chester. Thank you for
modeling what it looks like to love like Jesus.

Acknowledgments

Thanks to Karen and Dave Greer
for the fun dinner-out-brainstorming session!
You both are such a gift in so many ways!
I also want to thank Gus Krajicek for answering
my plethora of farming and harvesting questions,
my agent, Tamela Hancock Murray, for keeping
my fingers typing and my wonderful editor,
Melissa Endlich, for helping each of my stories
become as strong as possible. I learn so much
from each round of edits!

Chapter One

Daria checked the time again. One o'clock on a Friday afternoon, and not a customer in sight. Had the youth group from Calvary Ranch decided not to come? Maybe she should've offered a reduced rate. In her desperation for bookings, she nearly had. The only thing that had stopped her was she was worried word might get out and others might expect the same discount. She was barely keeping this business alive as it was.

Some less-than-supportive friends had suggested she'd made a mistake purchasing Off Roadin' It Adventure Rentals. She refused to believe that, or to give up on her dream. She'd loved riding off-road vehicles as a kid.

The two summers she and her sister spent with the Hamiltons, their fifth of eight foster families, held some of her most memorable moments. Like the first time she'd milked a cow or gone crawdadding. That had been a unique and hilarious experience. She laughed, remembering her sister's wide-eyed expression upon seeing the small lobster-like creature with its protruding beady eyes. *You mean we're going to eat them?* she'd squeaked.

Daria frowned as a familiar ache filled her chest. "I miss you, sis."

Sometimes her grief was so intense, she struggled to think straight. But then she'd catch a glimpse of her eighteen-month-old niece as she chased after a Texas grasshopper, or listened to her five-year-old nephew recite every conceivable T. rex fact documented, and joy helped lessen the sting. Boy, did she love those kids, and she was determined to give them the type of life they deserved. They'd been through so much, losing their mother and then moving halfway across the country to live with an aunt they usually saw once a quarter, if that.

If not for her housemate, Lucy Carr, the only foster parent Daria had ever called mom, Daria didn't know what she'd do.

A firm knock on her office door startled her. A deep-voiced *hello* followed. The man did *not* sound happy.

Had someone scheduled a tour she'd forgotten about?

"One moment, please." She jiggled her computer mouse and quickly clicked to her rental calendar. Other than the *maybe* highlighted in pink for the Calvary Ranch group, the day was blank. Unless she'd failed to enter something. With all her brain had been juggling lately, she wouldn't be surprised.

Slipping her cell phone into her pocket, she straightened her spine and stepped outside.

Her breath caught as her gaze landed on the tall, broad-shouldered cowboy standing in front of her. Dressed in faded blue jeans, gray hat and boots, and a green-and-blue checked shirt, he was good looking enough to land on the cover of a magazine. His aqua-colored eyes widened slightly beneath his thick, furrowed brows. He flicked a glance past her before narrowing his gaze on her once again.

She wasn't sure what caused her stomach to tumble

the most—the man's rugged good looks or the firm set of his jaw. Clearly, something had upset him.

"Welcome to Off Roadin' It Adventure Rentals." Rotating her bracelet, she donned her best smile, although it wobbled beneath the handsome man's stare. "How can I help you?" The mid-June air felt thick and sticky even for Sage Creek, Texas.

"The owner around?" He shifted, looked toward the rusted metal shop to the left, made a visual scan of the tree-dotted landscape across the lot, and then faced her once again.

"That's me. How can I help you?"

He studied her for a moment, as if processing her words. "You from around here?"

She stiffened. "I don't live on the property, if that's what you mean." His question struck her as odd and almost as if he meant to imply that she was an outsider. She'd heard people in small towns could feel distrustful of newcomers.

Thankfully, that hadn't been her experience with Sage Creek residents. Yet.

The cowboy shoved a hand in his pocket. "Seems you need to keep a better eye on your renters. To make sure they aren't riding all over the place, tearing up folks' land."

"I don't know what you mean, sir." Her clients stuck to her clearly marked map. She made sure of it, even if her trails had shrunk drastically from the hundred-plus acres that had once belonged to Omar, the former owner, before he sold off a chunk of his land.

"Did you rent your vehicles to a group of teenagers earlier this week?"

She swallowed. "College students. On Wednesday." Had they done something to upset the locals? She'd worried about that group, not because they'd demon-

strated even a hint of irresponsibility. But she remembered enough of her university days to know how rowdy
a bunch of frat boys, which they'd appeared to be, could
behave.

"You can't let kids go riding wild and unsupervised.
Isn't that illegal or something?"

"They were all of age." Even so, she'd emphasized and
repeated the rules multiple times before handing over the
vehicles' keys. Stay on the clearly marked paths. Don't go
over twenty-five miles per hour except on the back roads
connecting one trail to the next. And when they came to
the Reyeses' property, watch out for cows and chickens.
She'd anticipated the guys might ignore her speed-limit
rule but not the other boundaries.

"Then maybe you need to up your age requirements.
Or chaperone your younger clientele."

"Was there a problem?" Everything had seemed all
right when her customers had returned.

With a snort, the cowboy repositioned his hat, reveal-
ing spiked golden hair streaked with ginger. "I'd say. They
did doughnuts in my mama's strawberry patch. Plus, they
damaged a section of fence. Her cows could've gotten
out and damaged someone else's property or caused a
car accident."

She knew fence repair wasn't cheap, especially if a
person had to hire someone else to do it. Thank goodness, she maintained great liability insurance, an expensive preventative measure she bemoaned whenever she
wrote the check. Yet, if what this man said was true,
an animal could have broken free from someone's land,
and she could face quite the lawsuit. One big enough to
shut her down.

Wait a minute. "I would expect that to damage my vehicles." She turned and led the way down the short gravel

path to where she parked her equipment. Shielding her eyes from the glare of the midafternoon sun, she leaned in for close inspection.

"If they hit a post, maybe. They mangled the barbed wire."

Unfortunately, the paint, although still the characteristic neon green, held at least a decade's worth of scrapes and scratches. There was no way to prove what had caused the marks, unless... "Did you see any paint on the barbs?" For all they knew, someone else—a rambunctious teen on a neighboring farm or even a two-thousand-pound bull, for that matter—could have caused the damage.

"Didn't feel the need to investigate that closely."

She started to make a sarcastic remark but caught herself just in time. She drew in a slow, deep breath to defuse her defensiveness. "I can understand why you're upset, but what makes you think my customers were to blame?"

"Besides the tire tracks? An eyewitness saw them boys gallivanting about in vehicles painted just like the ones you got over there." He jerked his thumb in that direction.

A jolt of adrenaline triggered a wave of nausea. "Where's your property?"

"My mom's farm sits between you and the lake."

Her jaw went slack. "Ann Reyes?"

He gave a firm nod.

She and Ann were friends. Certainly close enough that the woman would speak to Daria personally if she had a concern. And yet she'd sent her son?

Before she could respond, her cell rang. She pulled it from her pocket and glanced at the return number. Kendra, her in-home day-care provider. She wouldn't be calling unless it was about something important. "I apologize, but I need to take this."

The man frowned but made a go-ahead motion.

She answered. "Hello?"

"Ms. Ellis, I hate to bother you in the middle of your workday, but Nolan's acting up."

She closed her eyes and pinched the bridge of her nose. Not again. "In what way?"

"He's been mouthy all morning, refusing to do as he's told, yelling when he doesn't get his way. Then during outside playtime, he became aggressive, taking bouncy balls from the other kids. And he pushed one of the little ones off a tricycle. She fell backward and smacked her head on the ground. I'm going to have to fill out an incident report, which looks bad on me."

Daria glanced back at Ann's son to find him watching her, as if trying to decipher her conversation. This wasn't a discussion she wanted to have in front of him, and the deepening crevice between his brows told her he wasn't pleased with the disruption.

She rubbed her temple. "I can only imagine how stressful he must have made things. I want you to know I take your concerns seriously and would love to talk about this further. Is this evening—"

"We're beyond that."

"I don't understand."

"The other parents have been complaining."

"And their children never act up?" Her tone held more bite than she intended. She exhaled. "I didn't mean to snap at you like that. I know you're simply trying to honor your other families." At the expense of hers? "Nolan just needs more time—"

"Look, I feel for you all. I hope you know I didn't make this decision lightly, but I can't afford to lose any children."

"I understand." She suppressed a sigh.

Surely, Kendra wouldn't kick Nolan out of day care.

How could Daria explain this to him in a way that his already wounded heart wouldn't view as rejection?

At least she worked for herself and therefore could adapt her schedule to some degree. Thankfully, Lucy was off for the next few days and would be able to watch the kids. That'd give Daria some time, although not much, to find alternate arrangements.

A child started crying in the background, and Kendra mumbled something Daria didn't quite catch.

"I'll gather the children's things and will expect to see you within the half hour."

The line went dead. Daria blinked, trying to give her brain time to catch up.

"Ma'am?"

She turned to the cowboy standing beside her, his expression now holding more concern than frustration. "Unfortunately, I'm going to have to finish this conversation later," she said.

"Wait a minute—"

"I'm sorry. Truly." Leaving her office door open behind her, she dashed inside for her purse and keys. "I'll stop by your mom's property as soon as I can."

"Yeah, and when will that be?"

"In an hour. Two tops."

Based on his expression, he was far from pleased with her answer.

Tyler watched the cute little brunette, maybe five foot three and a buck-twenty-plus-change, climb into her yellow two-door, cast a glance back at him over her shoulder, and then drive away. She seemed completely unconcerned about the destruction caused by her customers.

He hadn't even caught her name. If she thought she could avoid him or paying for damages, she was in for a surprise. His mom had enough to deal with trying to run her rapidly declining farm without other people taking advantage of her.

Dirt, gravel, and twigs crunched beneath his boots as he made his way to his vehicle. Inside, the smell of fries left over from the night before reminded him that he'd missed lunch. Then again, that was life on the farm, especially during harvest season. A man could work from sunup to sundown and still land two fields and a hay bale behind.

Turning the key in the ignition, he glanced back at the shack-like office building behind him. This place had been around about as long as he had. Although Tyler never would've called it thriving, Omar had always run it well. Tyler had to admit the new owner was much more pleasant to look at.

He smiled to himself, envisioning the soft contours of her heart-shaped face and the way the afternoon sun brought out the highlights in her sleek brown hair. Her dark brown eyes held a hint of innocence he found disarming, and maybe a shadow of sorrow.

For a moment there, he'd thought she might cry.

He frowned. He'd spoken more harshly than he'd intended. In truth, the frustration her clients had caused were but a small portion of his mom's problems. Issues that might never have occurred had he stuck around rather than enlisting in the military as soon as he'd come of age, and then reupping whenever he got the chance.

He couldn't help but feel as if he'd abandoned her for the past twelve years, and therefore was partially to blame for the state of her farm. But he was here now, and he planned to do everything he could to set things right.

Honestly, she needed to sell. List the property, pay off her debts, and then follow him to Nebraska. He had less than a month to fix her place up and convince her to get out from under it before it buried her. The fact that they were nearly two weeks behind harvest, thanks to extended heavy rains and soggy fields, certainly didn't help matters.

After running a few errands in town, he returned to the farm to find his brother gone—no surprise there—and his mom in the kitchen. With her lipstick and impeccably styled, shoulder-length silver hair, she appeared more suited for an office than farm work. Apron tied around a pink wrinkle-free blouse, she'd spread various baking ingredients and tools across the counter to her right and pantry items to her left.

Deep cleaning and making sweets? Not a good sign. Some folks shut down when they felt overwhelmed. Others, like his mom, started pulling out old recipes. Either that or began a massive decluttering campaign she inevitably never finished.

The fact that she was doing both simultaneously?

"What's all this?" He picked up a rusted dinosaur-shaped cake pan on the table that his mom had used for his eighth birthday.

"Just getting ready for the farmer's market."

"I see." The scent of vanilla wafted toward him. "Listen, I was making my way around the fence line today, checking what needs to be repaired and replaced, and I noticed a damaged section. I figured maybe some local teenagers had wreaked havoc, but Uncle Jed said he saw some college kids gallivanting about on off-highway vehicles."

His father's friend had long been considered close enough to be called kin. He was also one of the more successful farmers in the area, and therefore a fella worth listening to.

"Uh-huh?" She poured a spoonful of something into a large mixing bowl.

"He pointed me to Off Roadin' It Adventure Rentals, so I talked with the new owner."

"Such a nice lady, isn't she? And quite beautiful, I might add. Single, too." She shot him a mischievous grin.

His face heated. Outside, the hum of an engine and the sound of gravel beneath tires indicated company.

The twinkle in his mother's eyes increased, suggesting she thought, or hoped, this conversation was heading in an entirely other direction. She raised on her tiptoes to peer out the kitchen window. "Speaking of…" Smiling, she took off her apron, folded it, and placed it on the table. "Come with me." Primping her hair, she headed toward the entryway.

She paused and studied him a moment before brushing dust or maybe horsehair off his shirt. She then opened the door to reveal the pretty lady from Off Roadin' It Adventure Rentals. The woman held a toddler in her arms. Another child, who appeared to be four or five, stood beside her scowling. The two children had big brown eyes, the younger with sleek hair like her mother's, the older with soft curls long enough to create something of a halo around his head.

"Daria, honey, so good to see you." His mom enveloped the woman in a hug, the toddler sandwiched between them. Placing her hands on either side of the child's plump-cheeked face, she kissed her forehead. "How are you, sweet pea?" She greeted the boy with an equally enthusiastic embrace. The grandmotherly gesture softened the kid's scowl. "Y'all are just in time for some fresh-baked white chocolate chip macadamia nut cookies."

As if on cue, the oven timer beeped.

"Please forgive me for the mess." His mom ushered

her guests inside and toward the kitchen. "I'm reorganizing." She paused in the archway separating the living room from the kitchen. "I hear you've met my son Tyler?" The glint in her eyes made him nervous.

"In a way, yes, ma'am." The woman's gaze faltered.

He frowned, remembering how frustrated he'd been when he'd confronted her. He hadn't even given her a chance to tell her side of things. Then again, she'd been the one to hightail it out of there.

"But we weren't properly introduced." Tyler tipped his hat at her. "Ma'am."

"This is Daria." His mom began clearing space at the table. "She moved here, what, six months ago? And these two cutie-pies are Isla—" she ran her hand across the toddler's head "—and Nolan, my big helper. Isn't that right?"

The boy shrugged, his face downcast.

"Looks like someone's had a rough day." Tyler's mom bopped him on the nose. "Nothing some freshly baked treats won't fix, I hope."

The child released a gust of air, his gaze locked on a box filled with keepsake teaspoons Tyler's mom had collected over the years. "I can't go to day care."

"Oh, sweetie." Tyler's mom gave his hand a squeeze. "Tomorrow's another day."

He shook his head. "Miss Kendra don't like me uncuz I get so angry and don't use my inside voice or gentle hands."

Daria sighed, pulled out a chair, and sat while Isla occupied herself with a pile of food storage containers spilled across the floor. Daria relayed a conversation he assumed had been the reason she'd cut his visit short when he'd gone to confront her.

Sounded to him like her kid hadn't learned to regulate his emotions. Maybe he was given too much leeway or time alone.

Tyler looked at the woman's hand fiddling with a frog-shaped saltshaker. No wedding ring. It couldn't be easy raising two kids, a toddler especially, while trying to run a business. He should probably cut her some slack. Still he needed to express his concern and stress how important it was she better instruct her clients. He wouldn't make her pay for the damages.

Truth was, the section of fence those vehicles had ploughed through had been in poor shape to begin with. Half the wooden posts on this property were rotted. The best thing to do would be to yank them up and drive in something new. But with all that needed to be done around this place and his short time in Sage Creek, he had to prioritize, deal with the must-fixes, and hope the rest didn't turn off potential buyers.

"At least I can bring them to work with me when I need to." Daria's gaze flicked to his, sending a jolt through him before it returned to the hodge-podge assortment of gadgets shoved to the center of the table. "But that's not why I'm here."

"Oh?" His mom grabbed three tall glasses and two plastic cups, one with a sippy cover he was surprised she'd kept around.

"I wanted to apologize for the damage to your property. And to let you know that I plan to fix what I can and pay for whatever I can't. Like your strawberries."

"Don't you worry about that none." Tyler's mom placed cookies, two each, on saucers that she distributed, along with the milk, around the table. "I've got my strong boys here now. Might as well put them to use, right, Tyler?"

As if he spent his time eating pizza and watching television. But he gave a quick nod. "Won't be a problem, so long as this won't happen again."

Daria's expression fell, as if she felt chastised, but then she straightened and lifted her chin. "I want to do what I can."

He sensed this was important to her, and he admired her for that. "I understand. But digging up fence posts isn't easy. It takes more than a little elbow grease."

"How about y'all work on that together?" The way his mom smiled suggested she was hoping for more than repairs. Was she seriously trying to play matchmaker right now?

Unfortunately, the two were talking days and times before he could politely decline Daria's offer.

His mom looked rather pleased with herself as she buzzed about the kitchen, jabbering like she did when she got excited about something.

Did she think she would convince him to stick around if he fell for the woman? She knew he had a job waiting for him in Omaha. Not to mention he closed on his house in two weeks.

He wasn't going to redirect his life for a woman, no matter how beautiful she was.

Chapter Two

Daria released a breath, and the tension seeped from her shoulders. Ann's kitchen, with its periwinkle cabinets and open shelves lined with mason jars of flour, sugar, and other staples always soothed her. Light poured through the curtainless window above the sink and cast long rays across the floor, creating shadows in its deep, uneven cracks.

Coffee mugs and wooden spoons rested in the drying rack to the left of the apron sink. To the right, fresh-cut wildflowers occupied a lumpy ceramic vase, likely made years ago by one of Ann's sons. Above that, Ann kept dishes of various sizes, and an overflowing bowl of fruit sat on the far end of the counter.

Milk gone, Tyler grabbed his glass and stood. "Mom said you've been here six months?"

She nodded. "Just in time to enjoy your much milder winter."

"She's from Chicago." His mom gathered their empty plates and placed them in the sink.

"Really?" He pulled a jug of milk from the fridge, refilled his glass halfway, and returned to the table.

"Just north of Chicago, in a suburb called Wilmette."

"Came in time to miss blizzard season, huh?"

She nodded. "The day I left, it'd dipped below freezing, not counting the windchill. Simply walking from your car into the grocery store was practically unbearable."

"Guess our climate seemed like pretty near swimming weather." Tyler chuckled.

She smiled. "Almost."

This was a more pleasant side to Tyler than she'd encountered at her ATV rental. Not that she could blame him for his frustrations. He'd clearly only been looking out for his mom. She respected that, especially considering the rough go Ann had experienced recently. Daria could only imagine the pain the poor woman must've experienced when, less than a year ago, her husband of thirty-five years walked out on her, leaving her to run this place all alone. At least Tyler and his brother were here now.

"Me simming?" Isla gazed up with such big, brown eyes that Daria felt an urge to sweep her into a hug.

Ann beat her to it. She planted such a firm kiss on the kiddo's cheek, her face squished sideways. "You do? And where do you go swimming, love?"

"My home."

"You mean your yard, sweet pea?" Ann asked.

Isla shook her head, her pudgy arms crossed. "Inside."

"Really, now?" Tyler, clearly amused, regarded the child with a raised brow. "I could tell right away you were a princess. Should've figured you've got a palace hidden in the woods somewhere."

Daria was touched by his tenderness toward her niece. "She's referring to the bath, where I take her swimming every night. That was about the only way I could get her into the tub at first." She laughed. "Now I can hardly get her out."

Tyler chuckled, popped the last of his fourth cookie into his mouth, and then brushed the crumbs from his fingers. "So what brought you to Sage Creek, other than our above-freezing winters and hotter-than-an-over-cranked-sauna summers?"

"Lucy Carr." A lump lodged in her throat as she thought about the gentleness and compassion Lucy had shown her during the phone conversation they had shortly before Daria came to Sage Creek. Lucy hadn't pushed Daria to talk and had patiently waited through the long moments of silence. "My sister died in a car accident seven months ago. The kids' fathers—they've each got different dads—weren't in the picture, so I took in the children." She motioned to her niece and nephew.

Nolan, who'd joined his sister on the floor, was playing with some wooden contraption with a long handle on one end and two on the other.

"I'm sorry for your loss." The green in Tyler's aqua eyes looked more pronounced in the soft kitchen lighting.

"I appreciate that." She cleared her throat. "I adore the kids, but I'd never had them for more than a weekend and didn't have a clue how to parent. I knew I needed help and support." She'd been afraid to ask for it, though. Why, she wasn't sure, except maybe that vulnerability inherently came with the risk of rejection. While Lucy had proven she'd never turn Daria away, old wounds tended to cloud her thinking. "Lucy had talked so much about how great Sage Creek is."

Ann smiled. "We're all awful grateful to have her back." She glanced at Tyler. "You might not remember Lucy. She moved away when you were young. Came back about ten years ago to care for her mama once she started showing signs of dementia. Her daddy died the year before."

"She taught my Sunday school class one summer."

His mom nodded. "Pretty sure that sweet woman left an impact on every child in Sage Creek from your generation on."

On two hurting teens from the Chicago suburbs as well. If not for her former foster mom, Daria couldn't imagine—nor did she want to—where she might be now.

Everyone's eyes returned to Daria, as if expecting her to share more.

She pulled on a loose thread in her T-shirt hem, feeling a confusing mixture of being seen and exposed. "When Lucy invited me to move in with her, I knew that would be best for the children."

Lucy had been quick to sense and respond to Daria's unspoken yet desperate request.

"Nana Ann, what's this?" Nolan stood and approached her with a porcelain candleholder with two dogs and a cat encircling the base, paw in paw.

What he really meant was, "Can I have this?" although Daria kept that translation to herself.

"Well, now. I'd forgotten all about this little treasure." Ann's face lit up as if she was reliving a cherished memory. "Tyler here bought me this for Mother's Day one year with his own hard-earned money." She turned toward her son. "Asked your dad for extra chores, if I remember correctly."

"Yep."

"Considering how busy he kept you and your brother, I was quite impressed."

Tyler seemed to stiffen at the mention of his father. Because of how he'd treated Ann?

Nolan eyed the trinket with the same intensity as he did the candy in the checkout shelves at the grocery store. Then he set it on the floor and stood back up. "Has Cookie had her puppies yet?"

Ann took both his hands in hers. "Not last I saw her, although she's due any day now."

"Can we go see her?"

Ann looked at Daria, and she nodded.

"Yay!" Nolan began jumping up and down, fists pumping the air. Soon his sister joined him.

"Guess I best get back to work." Tyler stood and returned the hat he'd placed on the table to his head.

Ann, who had followed the children as they dashed for the front door, turned back around. "Think you could hold off just a bit? I'd like your help with something in your father's old barn of disarray."

Tyler hesitated, glanced at Daria, then back to his mom, his expression unreadable. "Yes, ma'am. Whatever you need."

"Thank you, honey. We'll stop there before searching for our little mama. That way you can get done whatever needs doing and then join us for supper." She shifted her warm gaze to Daria. "Y'all are staying, right? I've got way more leftover fried chicken than the three of us can eat, some croissants baked fresh today, and I can make a salad right quick with vegetables I picked fresh this morning. Unless you need to get back to the rentals?"

Lucy had her cultural meeting tonight, which meant Daria was alone with the kids. "Considering I don't have any rentals booked for this evening…"

Ann's eyebrows shot up. "Not a one?"

Daria released a heavy breath and shook her head.

"Oh, honey." Ann wrapped an arm around her shoulder and squeezed. "Things will pick up. I'm sure of it."

And if they don't?

Nolan's melodramatic grunting as he fought with the front door lightened her mood and reminded her that as challenging and painful as life had been lately, it'd been filled with incredible blessings as well. And those little nuggets were high on her blessings list, as were Lucy and Ann, the two women who treated her like a friend and daughter.

"Need help, little man?" Tyler came up beside him.

Isla, standing close by, resumed her bouncing while chanting, "Puppies! Puppies!"

Poor girl would be sorely disappointed when she realized the puppies remained tucked within their mama's belly. Hopefully, the dog and all the other farm sights and sounds would distract her. They normally just about sent the child's rapidly growing brain into sensory overload.

Descending the porch steps, Daria followed the others toward the well-trodden footpath leading to the neglected barn at the edge of the east pasture. The feather-topped grass, standing maybe two feet tall, swayed in the gentle breeze on either side of her, scenting the air with an earthy aroma.

As usual, Nolan raced ahead, pausing periodically to grab and throw a stone into the fields. Sweet Isla did her best to catch up, stumbling on occasion, and then clambering to her feet once again, almost every sense engaged.

Daria daydreamed about what it might be like to raise children at a place like this. With all the fresh air and exercise, time spent with the animals and digging in the dirt. Could her little business ever grow enough for her to afford such a thing? Nothing as elaborate as Ann's property, by any means, but maybe half an acre, some laying chickens, and a horse?

Her first goal was to get enough customers coming in to pay her monthly expenses. Then she needed to find reliable childcare for the days Lucy worked.

Ann reached the barn a moment after the children, pulled a key from her pocket, and unlatched the padlock. "Martin always insisted on guarding his junk." She rolled her eyes and slid open the massive door. "It's not like the coyotes are going to try to steal anything." She flicked on the light. "And yet here I am, bolting and un-bolting. Habit, I guess."

The bulbs positioned throughout the space, along with the light pouring in from the opened doorway and tall, glassless windows, eliminated some of the shadows and elongated others.

"Wow." With wide eyes, Nolan surveyed the as-sortment of items stacked on the dilapidated shelves lining the walls. Dusty odds and ends covered the long-abandoned stalls and filled the loft. "What is this stuff?"

"A bunch of rubbish that should've found its way to the dump decades ago." Ann ruffled Nolan's hair. "Al-though there are a couple items buried under all this mess that I need to find." She made eye contact with Tyler. "You remember your first saddle? And that old goat-tying dummy your dad built for you?"

"Considering I started riding when I was, what? Two?" He released a breath and rubbed the back of his neck, as if overwhelmed by the abundance of items. "Can't say I re-member anything about that, except for the stories you've told over the years. As to the goat-tying dummy..." He chuckled. "Yeah. I do remember that."

Daria glanced at her niece, who was scraping a twig through the dirt, and then looked back and forth between mother and son. She had heard enough stories to know Tyler had grown up fast and developed a fearless streak at a young age, apparently a trait his parents shared. Still, she couldn't imagine little Isla sitting on top of a five-foot, six-hundred-plus-pound horse.

Ann picked up a rusted watering can, turned it this way and that, and then set it back down. "The family just south of us asked to borrow that contraption. They want to try it out before they invest energy into making their own."

"Nana Ann?" Nolan peered up at her. "What's goat tying?"

"Best ask the master." She grinned and motioned to her son.

Dropping to one knee, Tyler placed a hand on Nolan's shoulder. "Goat tying is when a fella rides his horse into the arena, slides off when he reaches a tethered goat, and ties the critter's feet together as fast as he can."

Nolan's eyes widened, and he turned to Daria. "I want to do that."

His hope-filled expression about broke her heart—because there was no way she could afford anything even remotely related to horses or rodeo competitions.

She took his hand. "I'm sorry, sweetie, but that costs a lot of money."

"Not here it don't," Ann said.

"Yay!" Nolan resumed the jumping he'd done back at the house.

Daria wrinkled her brow. "I don't understand."

"Tyler here will teach him, won't you, son?"

Tyler's eyebrows shot up. "I...uh..."

Daria frowned, her cheeks heating. "I appreciate the offer, but really, we couldn't. I'd feel like we were taking advantage."

"I could! I could!" Nolan bounced on the balls of his feet.

Everyone laughed, but then Daria shook her head. "It's important to me to teach the children to be givers, not takers."

Mouth twisted to one side, Ann regarded her for a moment and then turned back toward the massive piles of randomness filling the barn. "Tell you what. If you help me clean out and sell all this here—" she looked at Nolan "—then Tyler will teach you goat tying."

"But he's never ridden a horse before." Daria's voice came out with a squeak.

"Everyone needs to start somewhere." Tyler winked at Nolan. "I can give little man some beginner lessons, no problem." A warm smile had replaced Tyler's overwhelmed expression, and Daria was tempted to think he might actually look forward to the prospect of teaching Nolan to ride.

Because of Nolan or her?

What a ridiculous question. The man was simply showing his mom respect and demonstrating the neighborly behavior for which the people of Sage Creek were known.

Everything Ann had shared about her son suggested he was an honorable, responsible, and fiercely loyal man. The fact that he was here now to look after his mom and help with the farm seemed to support Ann's claims.

She didn't remember Ann saying much about Tyler's personal life, but he was probably taken. Not that that was any of Daria's business, a fact she'd do well to remember.

With its mama standing close by in the stall, Tyler approached their newest foal from the left. As always, he began the training session with simple petting, checking for any sensitive places. He needed to build a bond that would translate into trust, and help the baby grow accustomed to handling. Because she was too young for treats, only ten days old, Tyler used gentle scratching as a positive reinforcement. Holding the lead rope in one hand, he reached across the baby's back to scratch her withers on her other side, intentionally laying his arm across her back in preparation for the day he'd saddle her. She responded by wiggling her lips, nibbling close to his hand.

He smiled. "You like that, huh, girl?" He rubbed the rope against the foal and loosely draped it around her neck, holding one end in his right hand and the other in his left on the foal's other side. This seemed to spook her, so Tyler released one end of the rope, allowing it to gently slip down the foal's legs as she stepped closer to her mom.

Tyler spent the rest of their time together introducing her to the halter. Afterward, he worked with the other babies and checked on their pregnant mares. Looked like his mom would have four foals to sell by the following spring. She'd diversified since his father left, which Tyler normally would've considered a good thing, only he didn't detect much in the way of long-term planning. Her attempts at growth seemed haphazard.

She needed to start liquidating, although convincing her of that wouldn't be easy. He'd hoped to initiate a conversation this evening over supper. That was before she'd invited Daria and her kids to join them.

The thought sent a jolt through his midsection, which startled him. What was that about? Granted, Daria was beautiful and kindhearted, if the way she responded to her niece and nephew were any indication. Clearly, she and his mom had developed a close enough relationship that his mom hadn't seemed embarrassed in the slightest by her messy kitchen. For that, he was grateful.

At the house, his brother's rusted and heavily dented pickup was parked next to his. The prodigal son had returned, hopefully ready to work and not loaf around on the sofa. Otherwise, that was another conversation Tyler planned to initiate.

Sighing, he climbed the porch steps, the weather-worn wood sagging beneath his weight. Inside, he set his hat on the entryway table and then followed the scent of warm croissants into the kitchen.

Everyone except his brother was gathered around the table. His mom was at the head with Daria to her right. Beside her, Isla sat in a high chair that looked old enough to have once belonged to him.

"Sorry I'm late." He crossed to the sink to wash his hands and then took an open seat that happened to be across from Daria. He glanced at her, and heat surged up his neck when their eyes locked. He cleared his throat and grabbed the salad bowl and tongs. "Wesley joining us tonight?"

His mom's gaze flicked to the archway at the living room entrance and then fell to her plate. "I imagine so, as long as he doesn't need to attend to other matters."

Like what? Feeding the animals or fixing the brakes on his mom's compact tractor? But asking that would only embarrass her.

"Did y'all ever find Cookie?" Tyler snatched a croissant from the basket in front of him, cracked it open, and slathered it with his mom's famous cinnamon butter.

Nolan's head bobbed up and down in an enthusiastic nod. "But not the babies, uncuz they need to get stronger in their mommy's tummy."

"Mama tummy," Isla parroted, patting her belly.

"Yes, of course." Suppressing a grin, Tyler matched the children's seriousness.

"I asked Aunt Daria if we could have one at our home, but she said no." He seemed unfazed by what must've felt like a heartbreaking denial. "Uncuz it's our house but not really our house, uncuz it's really Nana Lucy's house, and puppies like to chew things and make messes."

He snuck a glance at Daria. The twinkle in her eyes and the way her pink lips twitched toward a smile suggested she found the little guy as amusing as he did.

"But Nana Ann said we could keep my puppy here."

Nolan dipped a green bean in his ketchup, licked it off, and then dipped it again. "Then it can stay with his mama, uncuz otherwise he'd be sad, don't you think?"

"S'pose so." Tyler studied the little guy, worried about how he'd feel once his mom sold this place and all the animals. Maybe Daria would change her mind about Nolan bringing the dog home by then.

He picked up his chicken leg, and bits of the crispy coating fell back onto his plate. "How long have you known Lucy?" Seemed that woman formed a relationship with every mother, or surrogate, as was Daria's case, in Sage Creek and beyond.

A hint of a frown replaced Daria's otherwise quick smile, almost as if his question bothered her. "Since I was in the sixth grade." She shifted and stared down at her dinner plate, but then she lifted her chin and leveled her gaze. "Your mom said you were in the Navy?"

"Yes, ma'am. For twelve years."

"Did you enjoy it?"

"Some parts, like seeing new places and meeting new people, sure. It felt good knowing I was helping to preserve our freedom for folks back home. There were other aspects, however, like losing friends that had become like brothers…" His throat felt scratchy. He glanced at his mom. "That made a guy thankful for the people still around."

"Something smells good in here." Tyler's brother strode into the kitchen dressed in wrinkle-free slacks, a collared shirt and his hair shiny with some sort of hair product. He greeted everyone with a nod and then crossed to their mom. "Your famous croissants, huh?" He placed an arm around her shoulder and kissed her cheek.

Smiling, she patted his hand. "Join us."

He grabbed a croissant and a chicken drumstick. "Wish I could, but I've got things to attend to. Exciting things."

A hint of concern tightened her expression, but then she brightened. "I can't wait to hear all about it."

Tyler frowned. "You know there's still evening chores needing done. You planning on helping with those?" Based on Wesley's getup, that seemed unlikely. Nor had he done much before getting all snazzy, as far as Tyler could tell.

"Pretty sure the animals will still be here when I return."

Tyler's grip tightened on his fork. "That sounds pretty noncommittal to me."

"Boys." Their mom's tone was low but firm, her message clear. No conflict at the dinner table, especially not in front of guests.

She was right. This was a conversation Tyler needed to have with his mom and his brother, separately and privately. He would *not* let Wesley take advantage of her or make her life more difficult. History told him that was exactly what would happen if he didn't make his concerns known.

Then again, maybe this was a battle that didn't need to be fought, not if he convinced his mom to sell.

Turning back toward the table, he focused on the otherwise pleasant meal and even more enjoyable company.

His mom's friend intrigued him. The way she carried herself suggested an inner strength and determination undergirding her sweet and gentle demeanor.

The type of woman he might want to get to know better under different circumstances.

Chapter Three

Sitting at the back porch table, Daria inhaled the rich aroma of her heavily creamed coffee. "This is my kind of morning."

To her right, Nolan was creating a house from play-dough and twigs while his sister, squatting eye level with the middle deck railing, seemed mesmerized by an orange-brown caterpillar with white dots inching across the wood.

Lucy returned her bookmark to her devotional, closed it, and set it down. "I agree. Texas afternoons can melt the makeup straight off your face, but our days sure start out nice. What time do you figure you need to get going?"

"Your guess is as good as mine." She frowned. "Honestly, I don't understand why business is so slow. Based on Omar's previous sales numbers, last June held steady and increased through mid-August when school started again." He'd earned at least seventy-five percent of his annual profits during the summer. To survive the quieter winter months, she needed to do the same.

"Think it hurts that you're operating with less equipment, with some of your vehicles needing to be repaired and all?" Lucy asked.

"That might have turned away those wanting to ride as part of a bigger group."

"You just need to give those waiting for their turn something to do."

"Like what?"

Lucy wrapped both hands around her steaming mug. "I don't know. They can find plenty of ways to occupy their time once they reach the lake."

"True." Praise God, thanks to Ann, Daria still had access to the trails leading from her ATV facility to the county's most popular recreational areas. "But they have to get there and then bring their vehicles back before anyone else can use them."

"Right." Lucy tapped her chin. "You think you might want to try something else?"

Daria watched Nolan pull his sticks from his playdough and roll it in a ball. "Such as? I mean, Sage Creek doesn't exactly have a hopping job market. Besides, I really like the flexibility Off Roadin' It Adventure Rentals allows, and the fact that I can bring Nolan and Isla with me when necessary." That's what she would be doing next week if she hadn't found childcare. Once her business became strong enough, she could increase her one employee's hours to free more time for the kids. Maybe even hire a manager.

"Have you heard of geocaching?"

She nodded. "That's where people find treasures using coordinates of some sort and their phone's GPS, right? A great idea, except we don't have the best internet, and the signal gets weaker the farther you get from my office."

"I see. Well, what about an archery range?"

"Wouldn't I need open spaces for that?" She'd considered creating a course for dirt bike or ATV races, but she hadn't had time to research the idea further. "My property is pretty wooded, which is great for four wheeling, but the trees would probably get in the way of long-distance targets."

"So uproot some trees. Seems to me, as the business owner, you have the leeway to design the space however you need."

"I'm technically leasing to own, remember?" Although each month's payment earned her equity, the property wouldn't belong to her until Omar transferred the title. Still, Lucy's idea intrigued her. "What all do you think that would entail?"

"Don't know, but I can tell you who would." Her eyes held a teasing glint. "Tyler Reyes. Speaking of… How was dinner last night?"

Heat surged to Daria's cheeks, and she quickly looked away. "Fine. Good. I always enjoy spending time with Ann, and the children adore her."

"Uh-huh." Lucy gave a knowing smile. "And based on that blush of yours, I'm guessing you found her oldest son equally pleasant."

If by pleasant Lucy meant confusing and a bit unsettling. Daria wasn't sure what affected her most—his good looks or her uncertainty regarding how he felt about her using part of his mom's land. If he decided renting wasn't in Ann's best interests, Daria would be in a heap of trouble.

"Actually, my first impression…" She released a breath. "We had a bit of a rough start." She relayed how they'd met the day before.

"Watching out for his mama. Good man. Pretty sure he'll help you out, too, if you just ask. He could help with building an archery range, if you go that route, and he could probably fix some of your ATVs collecting dust in your shop."

Daria had to admit, that would be helpful. She paid the local mechanic, but he couldn't always fit her in. Lately, he hadn't had much time for her machines, but she didn't feel comfortable asking for help, let alone from the handsome cowboy, no matter how kind and gracious he appeared.

Her phone rang. She didn't recognize the number. Sitting straighter, she answered, "Off Roadin' It Adventure Rentals. How may I help you?"

"Hello. Do you have any openings this morning?"

What a great question to start her workday. "When are you thinking and for how many?" As if she had other bookings.

"I was hoping to bring my brother, nephews, and son. So five total. Two adults, two teens, and an eleven-year-old. Whenever you next have available."

"Front UTV drivers must be at least sixteen and have a valid driver's license. Passengers must be at least forty-six inches." She explained the rest of her rates and conditions and then held her breath, hoping her rules hadn't disqualified a potential customer.

"That sounds great. Any chance you can slide us in around 10:30?"

She checked her phone. It was 9:00 a.m. That gave her plenty of time. "Perfect."

Her next goal would be getting the party to book a full day. She'd discuss that option once they arrived and started filling out the necessary paperwork.

With a thumbs-up to Lucy, Daria rose and hurried inside for a pen and paper. Less than five minutes later, she'd jotted down his contact information, kissed the kids goodbye, and headed to work.

She called her mechanic en route to pester him about coming to fix the four-wheeler that was beginning to gather cobwebs. Unfortunately, she got his voice mail again. Massaging her temple, she left what must be her fourth message in the past two weeks.

She eased into Off Roadin' It Adventure Rentals's lot and parked close to the shop where she stored her vehicles at night, including those that were currently out of commission. One of them simply needed a new battery, which she'd asked the mechanic to bring with him when he came. *If* he ever came. The second most likely had a fuel system problem. She didn't have a clue what was wrong with the third.

Exiting her car, she was immediately accosted by the thick, sticky midmorning air that seemed to have increased a good ten degrees since she'd left Lucy's. Then again, she'd been sitting in the comfort of the house's shade. Unlike the pleasantly cooled home, her workshop, built from corrugated metal, lacked air-conditioning.

She heaved open the massive garage-style door with a grunt and stepped inside, inhaling the scent of dirt and motor oil. The sun streaming in created a large rectangular pattern across the earthen floor and reflected off her neon-green equipment.

She was in the process of easing her last running vehicle into the sun when the hum of an engine caught her attention. Wiping her hands on a rag, she turned to greet her customers.

Her breath caught at the sight of Tyler's aqua eyes and boyish grin. Driving a navy extended-bed pickup, he wore a gray T-shirt and his signature tan cowboy hat.

"Hey there." He rested his muscular arm on his opened window. "My mom sent me with these." He held up a basket of sweet breads packaged into individual servings. "Said you sell them to customers?"

She nodded. Although her sparse snack bar wasn't exactly a moneymaker, it helped keep her clientele happy and appeared to encourage Ann. It gave the older woman a reason to bake, and her baking seemed to help her cope with all the chaos and pain she'd experienced.

"You need a hand?"

Honest answer? "What I need is a mechanic willing to make house, or business, calls, preferably at a price I can afford." She gave an exasperated laugh.

"Then you're in luck, because engines are my specialty." Grinning, he eased onto the grass to her right, cut the engine, and got out.

"Really?"

He stood by her side. "In the Navy, I served as an aviation mechanic. Worked on fighter jets and whatnot."

"That sounds impressive." Handsome and handy? Such a combination could make a woman take notice. If she were looking for a relationship, which she was not. She had enough to manage building a new life for her niece and nephew.

"Just means I like working with my hands and fiddling with engines."

"I'm guessing they come in different sizes but are basically the same?"

"Something like that." Thumb in his belt loop, he eyed the vehicle. "Mind if I push this out into the sun?"

"Please. And thank you." A gust of wind swept her hair into her face. She brushed it out of the way. "What drew you to the military?"

"Needed something to do after high school, I guess. I enrolled as soon as I turned eighteen and went to boot camp the summer after my graduation. Just finished my last re-up."

In other words, he'd come directly to his mom's, likely because of her impending divorce. That said a lot about his heart, his loyalty and integrity. Although she got the sense he hadn't been around much in the decade-plus prior. Why was that?

How long was he planning to stay? She only asked out of concern for Ann, not because her pulse elevated whenever the cowboy came around.

He rubbed the back of his neck as he looked over the four-wheeler. "What's it doing? Can you get it to start?"

"Yeah. It runs for a bit but then sputters and dies."

"Sounds like a problem with fuel flow."

"Is that expensive?"

"Nah. If that's the issue, it should be easy enough to fix. You probably just have a clogged float needle or fuel filter. The hose could be kinked, too."

She released a heavy breath. "Awesome. Thank you."

"No problem."

Maybe he wasn't so opposed to her being here, after all. Then again, there was a big difference between acting neighborly to a small business owner and wanting her to use his family's land.

"Hold on." He dashed to his truck and returned with a toolbox from the pickup bed.

Two vehicles pulled into the lot, one after the other, most likely her renters.

Fiddling with her flower-shaped earring, she turned back toward Tyler. "I'm sorry, but I—"

He waved a hand. "I've got this. You go. Take care of business."

His easy smile halted her thoughts.

"Tyler Reyes? Dude!"

Daria startled at the deep-throated voice. She turned to see a tall, lanky man strolling toward them with a massive grin. The rest of his party lingered near their vehicles, talking, spraying sunscreen, and gathering their things.

"My man." Tyler stepped forward and embraced the guy in a man hug that ended with a fist bump to his back. "How you been?"

"'Bout same as always."

"Except you're a family man now? Those your kids?"

His friend nodded. "Step, but yeah. You working for Omar?"

Tyler shook his head, briefly explained Daria's role to his friend Luis, and introduced them to one another.

By then, Luis's family had joined them and he updated Tyler regarding the status of joint acquaintances. Soon, Tyler was sharing some of the places he'd been since high school graduation. He'd certainly traveled the world. He was also clearly a dedicated, determined, and self-controlled man who seemed to know what he wanted and how to go after it. Only not in a cutthroat type way, if how he talked about the people he'd served with was any indication.

She admired that.

Hands in his pockets, Luis widened his stance. "We should get together sometime. I'm hanging with family through Sunday." He motioned to the others with a tilt of his head. "Then I'm out of town for five days or so, but maybe after that?"

Tyler scratched his jaw. "Wish I could, but I'll only be in town for the next two weeks."

Why did his statement give Daria a twinge of disappointment?

"No problem," Luis said. "When do you plan on getting back?"

Tyler shrugged. "I got a job lined up in Omaha—working for the railroad."

"Guess me and the missus best have you out for burgers before then, huh? Could get the old crew together, too."

"Sure. Just give me a call."

The two exchanged numbers, then Luis glanced at the others. "Well, boys, what do you say? Ready to tear up some trails?" He shifted toward Daria. "That is, if you're ready for us."

She turned to Tyler. "Give me a minute to get them set up?"

"Go ahead." He waved her off, flashing a casual smile that stalled her breath. "I'll manage things here."

"I really appreciate this." And him. She might appreciate him a little too much, considering the effect he seemed to have on her. She turned to the others with her most enthusiastic smile. "Let's get you all taken care of."

Leaving Tyler to fix the problem elevating her stress, she led her customers to the small shack-like structure that housed her office. What she really wanted to do was stay and watch, if only to learn more about him.

Which was totally ridiculous, especially since she'd just learned he'd be gone soon.

Squatting in front of his opened toolbox, Tyler watched Daria walk away with a captivating mix of confidence and approachability. Dressed in high-waisted jeans and a light yellow T-shirt that brought out the pink undertones in her skin, she had a beauty that accelerated his pulse. Her smile, with the hint of a dimple to the right of her mouth, and the way her eyes had lit up when he'd offered to check out her quad, about stole his common sense.

Hopefully, one of these days, once he got settled in Omaha, he'd find someone to build a life with. Someone to share the most exciting and mundane parts of his day and build mutual dreams regarding the future.

Like the sound of little feet running through the house.

An old phrase his now deceased grandmother used to repeat came to mind: *All in God's timing.*

True, but Tyler figured it would help things along if he stayed in one place long enough to get to know a lady. Preferably someone with the same tenderness and gumption he saw in Daria.

Shaking the thought aside, he grabbed his phone and navigated to his favorite agricultural online radio. Unfortunately, the wheat market hadn't bounced back like his mom had hoped. Based on the rules of supply and demand, per-bushel prices would only decrease as other farmers brought their grain to the elevators. If only his mother had contracted forward. He still didn't understand why she hadn't, except that she seemed to spin in circles when overwhelmed.

Lord, we could sure use some hot, dry temps and a steady wind to dry out our fields right about now.

Working the land sure could get a man praying. Few people understood complete dependence on God and the rain He sent quite like a farmer.

He clicked to the country music station and set to work on Daria's ATV. He was just returning the carburetor to the vehicle when she returned with Luis and the others. She explained, in detail, a series of rules, emphasizing where the guys could and couldn't ride. If she'd given those rowdy college kids the same spiel, they bore the sole blame for the damage to his mom's farm. Then again, she might have course corrected after what happened.

He appreciated her efforts either way.

After sending Luis and his crew off, she turned to face him, hands on her hips. "Good news I hope?"

"Yep. If by that you mean it won't cost you a dime."

"Seriously?" Her expression registered a mixture of hope and caution.

He nodded and wiped the dust from his hands. "Nothing more than a clogged fuel line. I blew it out with my air compressor."

"That you just happened to have on hand, I take it?"

Her teasing made him chuckle. "Seems so."

"I can't tell you how relieved I am to know I won't be spending more money on an unexpected expense."

He frowned. "Omar leave you with a mess?" That didn't seem like him, but he was getting on in years.

"I wouldn't say that, exactly."

That sounded like a noncommittal response. Maybe Omar had lost some of his attention to detail or the energy to run this place like he once had. Didn't make it right, but at least Tyler could understand that. Just look at his mom's farm. She'd let it fall into disarray as well. They'd simply have to make sure their sell price reflected that. Hopefully, she wouldn't walk away carrying a load of debt with her.

They'd have to deal with that if and when that time came.

He shifted his weight. "You need me to look at anything else?"

"Actually… Do you know anything about archery?" She explained what she wanted help with.

"A range, huh?" He shifted toward the wooded area his friend and his family had just disappeared into, trying to remember the terrain. "All your land treed?"

"Unfortunately, most of it, yeah."

"Acreage clearing doesn't come cheap."

"I kind of figured." Poor woman looked like he'd just told her she was about to lose the business. If she didn't find an additional income stream, maybe she was. Apparently, she and his mom had more in common than he thought. No wonder they'd formed such a quick friendship. At least Tyler's mom could rely on his muscle and experience. Who did Daria have?

"Let's go take a look." He forced optimism into his voice.

Her face brightened. "Wonderful, thank you. Just give me a minute to grab a trail map."

"No problem."

She jogged off and returned a moment later with a clipboard and stubby pencil. "Figured I should probably take some notes."

"Makes sense."

He fell into step beside her as they made their way across the lot and onto the main trailhead. Wind rustled the leaves and a bullfrog croaked in the distance. "The creek's that way, right?"

She nodded. "I'm guessing you've been here before."

"Omar used to let my brother and I ride pretty much wherever we wanted during off-seasons. On our own quads, of course."

"What a fun childhood you must have had. Every kid should have such access to nature. I love that I can give that to Nolan and Isla. They grew up in the city, lived in an apartment complex surrounded by concrete and other buildings." She plucked a tiny yellow wildflower growing beside the path. "He loves it here. Likes to pretend he's a mountain man or something."

Tyler laughed.

They continued in silence, pebbles and branches crunching beneath their feet. A squirrel scampered across the path ahead of them and up a nearby tree. Filtering through the leaves, the sun dappled the ground with light.

"I can tell my mom enjoys spending time with Isla and

Nolan." He smacked a mosquito on his arm. "They're like the grandchildren she never had." Yet. Didn't have yet. "Your folks close?"

"My biological mom lives in Ohio." Her voice took on a biting tone, suggesting some deep wounds lay just beneath the surface.

"I didn't mean to pry." He'd heard city folk preferred to keep to themselves. Something to do with people wanting more privacy the less space they had between one another.

"You're fine. It's just…" She released a breath. "My sister and I were raised in the system."

What did that mean?

His confusion must have shown, because she added, "Foster kids."

"Oh. Wow. That must have been rough."

She shrugged. "Could've been worse." She paused at a T in the trail and propped fisted hands on her hips. "Heading west, it continues through more of what we've just walked through. It thins out some going eastward." She pointed in that direction. "Then on through a small slice of county-owned land before cutting through your family's property."

In other words, she wanted to change the subject. He understood that. As if losing her sister hadn't been painful enough, the poor woman had obviously endured a great deal in her life. Hardship like that could've turned her bitter or caused her to give up entirely.

And yet, here she was, fighting to give her niece and nephew the best life possible.

His admiration for her grew whenever they interacted. If he wasn't careful, when it came time for him to leave, his heart would be in a heap of trouble.

Chapter Four

Daria stopped when the path, made uneven by rocks, pot-holes, and exposed roots, reached a V. Shielding her eyes from the late-morning sun, she checked the time on her phone and then gazed down the trail in both directions.

The gentle breeze stirred the air with Tyler's leathery-citrus scent, making her all too aware of his presence beside her.

"What're you thinking?" he asked.

That I'm enjoying this time with you more than I should.

She eyed the printed map attached to her clipboard. "I'm trying to visualize the east side of my property. How much clear space do you think I'll need for an archery range?"

She wanted every foot of land available for a moto-cross course. Unfortunately, the two would not be compatible. The boulders, hills, and turns that made for great dirt biking or ATV competitions would lead to archer frustration and twisted ankles. The question was, which would be the most economical and provide the greatest chance of success?

"You hoping to accommodate kids and adults?"

She nodded.

"Then you'll want to allow for a minimum of twenty yards or so. Maybe more. Beginners can always step closer, but a lot of men will want to feel like your range helps prepare them for hunting."

"I might be able to swing that. There's a grassy section dotted with bushes I think might work." Ducking below some branches, she turned onto a narrow trail bordered by bushes and tall grass on either side.

He followed. "Might not be a bad idea to host competitions, if you're able."

A bird, it sounded like a warbler, sang in the distance. "That's an interesting idea. How big of an area would I need for that?"

"I'd suggest you shoot for anywhere between forty to eighty yards."

She tried to envision the distance in comparison to a football field. "You don't happen to know how much something like that would cost to clear, do you?"

"Not off the top of my head."

At this point, any expense felt like too much, especially since she wasn't entirely sure why her rentals were so low. She'd been blaming her lower-than-projected numbers on the fact that Omar had sold off part of his land. But what if she was the issue?

What if she didn't know how to effectively run a business? Then it wouldn't matter how many ideas she came up with.

"You okay?"

"Huh?" She glanced at Tyler to find him watching her with a concerned expression.

He moved a low-lying branch out of her way. "You seemed deep in thought."

She gave a halfhearted chuckle. "Just crunching numbers."

"You know, I helped plant some of these trees back in the day."

"You did?"

"For an Arbor Day event hosted by Omar." Tyler swatted at a crane fly buzzing near his face. "He got my principal to send the fourth, fifth, and sixth grade students. Probably his way of getting 'more bang for his buck,' as people say, in terms of free labor."

"Smart man."

"He was at that. Might even have gotten the school to pay for the saplings. Initially, we were told we could only plant one, to save enough for the older grades, but my buddies turned it into a competition to see who could finish first. We were done and bored before half the class finished digging their holes."

"Oh." She raised her brows in mock disapproval. "You were one of those kids, I see."

"If by that you mean ornery and overly energetic, absolutely." He flashed a grin.

"Your poor mother."

"There was a reason my folks started me goat tying so young. My mama said she'd been desperate to find a way to tucker me out."

Daria laughed. "Sounds like Nolan. He can get pretty riled up, especially if he eats too many sweets, something I wish his former day-care provider had paid more attention to."

"Is that why they kicked him out? Because he was too rowdy?"

"That didn't help. But I think most of his behavioral problems come from him missing his mom."

"That has to be rough. How much does he understand?"

"Of her death, you mean?"

He nodded.

"Not much, I don't think. Just that he wants to see her and she isn't here." Daria could relate. If only she had spent more time with her sister when she'd had the chance. Made sure she knew how loved she was. Considering how much Daria struggled with the loss of her sister, and everything that followed, it was no wonder that Nolan did as well. So much in his world had changed so rapidly, there was probably a good deal he couldn't possibly comprehend. She would've been more surprised if he hadn't acted up.

"Sorry your sitter wasn't more understanding."

"She was just trying to do what was best for her business." And not just in terms of appeasing the other parents. Although Kendra had originally been fine with taking Nolan and Isla a few days a week, she'd started pushing for full-time about two months ago. She probably had another family waiting, one that would pay her for the entire week.

"If only I could finagle a way to uproot some trees as economically as Omar planted them."

"Don't s'pose the county will let you use their land?"

"Doubt they'll want the liability." That reminded her that she needed to contact her insurance agent to see what kind of coverage she'd need for a thing like this. That alone could make her decision for her. She released a sigh. Why did everything have to be so complicated and expensive?

"I imagine all this feels pretty...frustrating."

Why did the compassion radiating from his eyes make her feel so vulnerable? Maybe because of all the mind games her ex-boyfriend used to play. He'd act like he cared one minute, only to use her emotions against her later.

But she sensed that Tyler was different.

How much of her perception came from the stories

she'd heard from Ann rather than her interactions with him? Honestly, she'd viewed him favorably before they'd even met.

And if not for Ann? If her and Tyler's paths had crossed at a coffee shop back in Chicago? She probably would've kept their conversation polite yet brief. *Hello. Excuse me. Goodbye.*

That was a major reason she was still single at twenty-eight. That and the fact that her last boyfriend had proven to be a jerk. If only she'd figured that out sooner, maybe she wouldn't have been so devastated by their breakup. Or surprised to learn he'd been cheating on her with a mutual friend.

"I really appreciate your time." She plucked a leaf from a branch and began tearing it along the veins. "I'm mainly exploring options at this point. If the archery range idea doesn't prove viable, I'll figure something out." She was much too committed to her dream for Nolan and Isla, for the life she intended to give them all, to give up easily.

"I like your gumption."

His praise heated her cheeks. What was it about this man that triggered such a response within her?

She was probably just in an emotionally vulnerable place.

Regardless, he'd be moving to Omaha soon enough. Considering how soon he'd be leaving Sage Creek, she'd be wise to learn as much about archery, or whatever outdoor adventure activity she landed on, as she could before he left.

She paused at the head of a footpath. "This is a short-cut to a stretch of land I think might have the most potential." She led the way under a natural archway made from entangled branches covered with vines and onto the less traveled path. They continued through a small, sun-scorched grassy area that reached knee high. They crossed over two slightly wider dirt paths that formed one oblong loop and stopped at the border of more grassland.

Tyler came up alongside her. "This area's what, over a hundred yards?"

"I'm not sure, but it's the biggest area I've got with the fewest trees."

He nodded, scanning the expanse before them. "Some bush-sized mesquites, one of them near dead as far as I can see. Those little jewels are pretty hardy, and their roots go deep, but I don't think you need to worry about them. Seems you've got plenty of open space for a range. 'Course, you'll probably want to get as close to exact yardage as possible. Folks, especially those practicing for a competition, will want to know."

She must have looked discouraged or perplexed, because he added, "I've got a measuring wheel you can use. Better yet, I can measure for you."

"I hate to put you out."

"Just let my buddies and I come shooting before I leave, and we'll call it good."

Right. He'd be gone soon, something she needed to remind herself of whenever he tossed her that playful grin of his.

He scanned the area on either side of them. "Do you have another way to get folks out here?"

"Unfortunately, other than on a mountain bike, no. Do you think people would mind coming the way we did?"

"Might get more business if you create easier access. Especially for those who are afraid of snakes."

"Like widening the path." She gave one quick nod. "You don't happen to know anything about motocross courses, do you?"

"You thinking of hosting a competition?" His frown suggested the idea displeased him.

Because he didn't think her capable? Maybe he worried she wouldn't be able to keep people off his mother's land. Unfortunately, there was probably a bit of truth to that. She could state rules clearly, post signs in numerous places, and even make participants sign an agreement. But she could not monitor whether or not they complied.

She shrugged. "Just trying to find the most economical and profitable option possible."

He studied her. "Your neighbors might not be so keen on that, although I suppose so long as you kept riders far from other people's fence lines and such." He scratched his chin. "I goofed around on a dirt bike some as a kid, but I never raced. I can probably help you brainstorm what all something like that might take and connect you with someone more knowledgeable to answer whatever questions I can't. How about we bring your map and paper and head to Wilma's to talk all this out?"

Wilma's? The diner? Why did the thought of sitting across a table from him send a quiver through her midsection? It wasn't like he was asking her out or anything, for goodness' sakes. The man was simply being considerate.

She shook her head and looked at the time on her phone. "I've already taken too much of your morning. Besides, your friend and his family could be heading back soon." Although she hoped they'd stay out all day. That was her hope with each rental, even those who came in with a definite time in mind. But her commitment to remain flexible also meant she needed to stick around to close people out once they finished.

"How about I call my buddy? See where he's at and when he anticipates getting back."

Her eyes widened. "Oh, no. I mean, thank you, but I don't want to bother my customers."

"Yeah. I should probably get back to the farm before any of our critters up and run away." He chuckled.

"The fence repair. I'm so sorry that I haven't made arrangements to come out. It's just—"

"No big deal. I figured weekends are your busiest days and that you won't be able to stop by for a bit."

"I can probably come tonight once I close up here. I imagine you want to get that section fixed before any of your mom's animals wander away."

"I'm sure you'll be plumb tuckered out after being in the sun all day. There's no rush on my end. We've got our horses and cows in a different pasture. We rotate to avoid overgrazing the land and turning it into a dust bowl."

She smiled. "I appreciate your grace, but your mom's property is a priority for me. I don't usually get a lot of customers after six. I'm also off on Monday. It's slow enough that I'm comfortable leaving my part-time—and only—employee in charge." The guy was the son of one of Lucy's friends. He was looking for a way to earn some extra cash and therefore willing to work sporadic hours for a reasonable rate.

Ugh. Lucy would be working. "I forgot I'll have the kids that day."

"Bring them. I can give Nolan his first riding lesson after."

"He can be a bit rambunctious." And disobedient, but she didn't want to label him that way. Like Lucy often used to say, usually to Daria's sister after a big mess-up, *You aren't your behavior. Your actions are symptoms of something deeper, sweet girl. Of a wound God's wanting to heal.*

"You're speaking to the king of rowdy himself."

She laughed. "So you're liable to go climbing trees, turn every twig into a sword or machete, and wander off when I'm not watching?"

"I might join the boy on an adventure or two." He winked, causing a jolt of electricity to shoot through her.

She turned toward the bike trail, face down to hide her blush. "You ready to head back?"

"Lead the way."

Silence stretched between them once again as she wrestled with the confusing emotions Tyler always seemed to evoke. Yes, he was handsome, and he was clearly a man of integrity, at least as far as Ann was concerned. He had spent a chunk of his morning hiking across her property in over eighty-degree weather when he surely had other tasks waiting back at the farm.

He was the type of man she might want to get to know better, if only he wasn't leaving.

Then again, maybe the fact that he was leaving made her attraction toward him feel safe. She couldn't get hurt by a man she'd spend such a short time around.

Tyler walked Daria back to her office and lingered a moment, making small talk—about his mom's baked goods, the weekly farmer's market, the antiques in his mom's barn of disarray, and the foals he was training. He'd already spent more time at Off Roadin' It than he'd expected, especially considering all he needed to do at the farm. So why did he feel so reluctant to leave?

That was a question he had no intention of entertaining.

Accompanying him to his truck, Daria paused on the way to grab two waters from a cooler outside her equipment storage area. She handed one to him. "I'll stop by as soon as possible."

"Whenever's best for you works for me." He hid a grin beneath an appropriately casual smile. "Hope you get a lot of rentals this afternoon." When they met to talk about her archery plans again, maybe he could help her brainstorm ways to increase her business. That was the neighborly thing to do, especially with her being his mom's friend and all.

He wasn't thinking of ways to help because he was attracted to her. Although he had to admit, she had the cutest little dimple just to the right of her mouth whenever she smiled. And the way her brows furrowed together when she was thinking hard on something...

Tyler, what are you doing?

Giving himself a mental shake, he climbed into his stuffy truck. The hot leather stung through his thin T-shirt, and a wasp landed on his windshield wiper then flew off.

Easing out of the parking lot, he cast one last glance at Daria through his rearview mirror and then turned on the quiet two-lane highway toward home.

Back at the farm, he was pleased to see his brother's vehicle in the same spot as before he'd left. Hopefully, Wesley had been working during that time and had mucked the stalls as Tyler had asked. Then Tyler could spend his afternoon unclogging their pond's drainage pipe before overflow caused erosion problems.

But first, some fuel.

He parked his truck between his brother's and an old tractor he planned to fix and sell and dashed inside for a couple of sandwiches and some sweet tea. The smell of garlicky beef and toasted bread drew him to the kitchen. His mom and brother sat at the table going through a stack of brochures.

"Tyler, you're just in time for lunch." His mom grabbed

her and his brother's dirty plates and stood. "Roast beef sandwich and potato salad sound okay?"

He greeted her with a kiss on her cheek. "Sounds delicious. But I can make my own."

She dismissed him with a flick of his hand. "It won't take me but a minute." She pulled various containers from the fridge and lined them on the counter. "How was our sweet friend Daria?" She glanced back at him over her shoulder, a playful glint in her eye.

Averting his gaze so she couldn't see the flush in his cheeks, he strode to the sink to wash his hands. "She was appreciative for the baked goods."

"You sure were gone for a spell. I was starting to wonder if I might need to send someone over there to fetch you."

"I helped her out a bit." Ignoring the insinuation in her tone, he explained how he'd spent the morning.

"I'm guessing that didn't put you out none."

He grabbed a glass from the cupboard, poured himself some iced sweet tea, gulped half of it down, and then refilled it. His mom snatched two slices of bread before he could.

Nudging him out of the way with her hip, she popped them into the toaster. "Go on, now. Have a seat. It's not every day I get to feed my two favorite men."

He chuckled, knowing there was no sense arguing, and that his mom received genuine joy from pampering those she loved.

"I appreciate it." He migrated to the table and sat across from his brother, who was jotting numbers onto a notepad. "What's all this."

Wesley looked up. "This, my friend, is what you call options."

"For?" Tyler picked up a library book titled *Agricultural Diversification*.

His mom brought him a plate loaded with more food than he could possibly eat. "I was reading an article in the *Modern Farmer* that talked about the benefits of diversifying, and they had a whole section on Dorper sheep. I had no idea how marketable those creatures are. They're tough, let me tell you. Mamas can give birth in the dead of winter, and within forty minutes, their babies are up nursing and walking around in the snow. Plus, they're not picky grazers and can share the same pasture as our cows."

He studied her with a wrinkled brow. "You're not thinking of adding more livestock, are you?" She needed to be selling whatever she could, not increasing her debt.

"I'm not sure exactly what I'll do. What we'll do." She motioned to him and his brother. "It's so nice to have you both here again." She gave Tyler's shoulder a squeeze. "Obviously, we can't do anything until we sell all our wheat, but I want to start learning all I can now, so I'm ready to invest smart when the time comes. Of course, we'll want to give ourselves plenty of time to get our property ready. Considering our fencing is set for large animals, I figure we'll need to redo, what, six miles or so?"

His brother gave a low whistle. "That'll keep a man busy. Speaking of investments…" He pushed back from the table and stood. "I best get changed for my meeting with FDM Financials."

Frowning, Tyler watched his brother amble out of the kitchen with his normal carefree swagger—as if the farm weren't in complete disarray and their mother wasn't heading toward a financial crisis.

"Is Dad's name still on this property?" Tyler asked.

She shook her head. "He signed it over as part of our mediation agreement."

In other words, he'd cut his losses and bailed before this place buried him. Smart man. Now to convince his mom to do the same. "We need to get a Realtor out here, find out what the property's worth and what all we need to do to get it ready to sell."

His mom stared at him as if his words hadn't quite sunk in, and for a moment, he thought she was going to cry, but then her face brightened. "Oh, sweetie. I can understand how overwhelming this must feel, coming back after having been gone for so long. I also know how hard you've been working and how much still needs to be done. Everything will work out. It always does."

Apparently not, otherwise this place wouldn't be in such a state. But he kept that observation to himself. "Please pray about selling." And the sooner the better. Otherwise, he feared she'd land in a financial mess too deep to climb out of.

"I couldn't possibly. I've already lost so much, and this property has been in my family for generations. You know that."

"Maybe you could rent it to other farmers." Then she'd actually stand a greater chance of holding on to it, because as things stood now, she was rapidly heading toward losing everything.

"This is my way of life." Moisture pooled in her eyes. "Maybe if you gave this place a chance, you'd find working the land isn't such a terrible way to spend your time."

"I did work the land. For eighteen years." He winced at her sharp intake of breath. "I'm sorry. I didn't mean to be unkind." How could he explain how he felt without causing her further pain? "It's just…this was never my dream. Besides, my railroad buddy vouched for me. I won't jeopardize his good name by bailing so close to my start date." It would take more than a summer to turn this place around. By then, his job offer would be long gone.

"God will make a way. Have faith, sweetie."

"What if all the problems you've experienced—the heavy rains, the still soggy land and falling wheat prices…" He wasn't sure what other issues she'd experienced, but he got the sense there were many more. "What if those are signs God wants you to sell?"

She didn't respond right away, and when she did, her voice was quiet and calm. "What if He brought you back to Sage Creek to help me save the farm?"

Her words hit him hard, reminding him of why she was in this position in the first place. Tyler's dad wasn't the only one to blame. What might have happened had Tyler stayed? The farm had never exactly been thriving, but they'd always made do. And what about her and his father's marriage? Had the stress of trying to maintain it all, just the two of them and whatever seasonal farm hands they managed to hire, created cracks in their relationship that eventually led to divorce?

He should've seen this coming. All of it. But he'd been too wrapped up in himself, too focused on running a thousand miles, literally, in the other direction to stop long enough to think about the damage he was leaving behind.

Unfortunately, there wasn't anything he could do about the past. He could, however, see that his mom was taken care of in the future. The only way he could do that was by moving her to Omaha with him. On a railroader's salary, he could easily support them both without worrying about too much or too little rain, falling grain markets, or wheat blight. Staying here would only dig the hole deeper for them both.

He'd pushed the subject far enough today. Hopefully, his mother would come to realize the logic in his advice. In the meantime, he'd pray that Christ would help her see that He still had so much good planned for her.

Maybe even, God willing, the addition of a daughter-in-law and a couple of grandkids one day.

He finished the last of his sandwich and washed it down with a swig of sweet tea. "Thank you for lunch. It was delicious."

His mom, who had begun cleaning up the counters, shot him a smile. "Of course. You working on the fence tonight?"

His thoughts sprang to Daria, causing his pulse to spike. "Yeah."

But not the section he and Daria would be working on, even though he could easily knock that out. He told himself he was simply giving her the opportunity to do the right thing—for her sake. And that his actions were in no way motivated by a desire to spend time with her.

She'd said she'd stop by, if no ATV renters came in. A prospect he should *not* find so appealing, and not only because her visit would indicate a lack of business.

He could easily fall for a woman like that. Then his mother wouldn't be the only one leaving a piece of her heart in Sage Creek.

Chapter Five

Sunday morning, Daria woke to the sound of Isla's chattering. Munchkin sat in her crib, occupying herself with her favorite stuffed animal. Daria couldn't make out all of Isla's words, although every once in a while, her "bye-bye" resounded clearly.

Daria glanced at the time on her phone and slipped out of bed. She crossed the room and stood over Isla's crib. "Look who's up." And well before 6:00 a.m. "Want to come snuggle with Auntie?"

She picked her up and turned back toward the bed.

Isla shook her head and looked around. Spotting the stack of books on Daria's bedside table, she reached toward them, opening and closing her chubby hand. "Stowy?"

Daria smiled, grabbed a book with a glittery fish on the cover, and gave Isla a squeeze. "I would love to read to you." Unexpected motherhood had come with many challenges, but it came with even more blessings. Like chubby-cheeked smiles and early-morning cuddles.

She slipped, with Isla, back into bed.

The child wiggled in closer, thumb in her mouth, and rested her head on Daria's chest. They made it through the book numerous times, Isla running her fingers across each texture, before Nolan wandered in. He was clutching a plastic pterodactyl as if it were a teddy bear.

"Hey, kiddo." Daria motioned him closer. "Want to join us?"

"I'm hungry."

"Me hungy! Me hungy!" Isla pushed Daria's arm away and slid to her feet. "Nummies pwease. Me nummies!" Repeating what was quickly becoming her favorite word, she tottered halfway across the room.

Daria laughed. "I'm coming."

Lucy appeared in the doorway wearing a plush purple robe and matching slippers. "How about I make us all some caterpillar pancakes?"

"Yeah!" Nolan grinned and dashed toward the kitchen, Isla following close behind.

"Morning." Lucy gave Daria a sideways squeeze. "Now might be a great time for you to jump in the shower."

She covered a yawn with her hand. "Good idea. Thank you."

They arrived at church two hours later with the kids fed and little hands and faces syrup free. Isla had insisted on bringing her pink stuffed monkey with its missing eye. Nolan scampered from the car with an armload of plastic dinosaurs. They probably helped him make friends with some of the other preschoolers at church.

Isla on her hip, Daria scanned the parking lot for Tyler's truck and immediately chided herself for it. She thought about that man way too much, especially considering he'd soon be gone.

Shaking the image of his boyish smile from her mind, she guided Nolan past the sanctuary and down the hall toward the classrooms in the back. Upon reaching the nursery, Isla wiggled and strained to get down. Once released, she toddled off toward a large, rainbow-colored blowup ball.

Lucy chuckled. "Looks like peanut's found her happy place."

Daria watched as a teen volunteer she'd come to recognize followed Isla to a box filled with dress-up items. "Both kids really seem to love it here. Too bad Nolan didn't settle in as easily at day care."

"Think it's because of the adult-to-child ratio?"

"I do love how many volunteers this church has, and how relaxed and engaged they are. They always seem so happy to see the children."

"Who wouldn't be excited to spend time with your pumpkins?" Lucy gazed down the hall with a vague expression that suggested she was deep in thought. She brightened and looped her arm through Daria's. "Come on. I know exactly who you need to talk to."

She whisked Daria past a handful of classrooms, out of the church, and across a short stretch of grass to the adjacent parish house. "I bet one of our high schoolers would love to watch your little ones a few days a week. They'd probably enjoy earning a little extra spending money, and the kiddos would get more love than they knew what to do with."

Daria smiled. "That would be amazing." Nolan would thrive with more focused attention.

Inside the parish house, laughter, conversation, and the smell of hot chocolate and cinnamon filled the small kitchen as teenagers dashed in and out to grab doughnuts or other treats. Enough sugary baked goods lined the counter to feed the entire church twice over, although the youth were making a significant dent.

Lucy glanced around. "Looks like the Owenses aren't here yet. They're the church's volunteer youth leaders of

Trinity Faith. They'll know which teens are looking for a job and who's most reliable."

While they waited, Lucy struck up a conversation with sixteen-year-old twin sisters with long auburn hair and a splattering of freckles on their cheeks, nose, and forehead. Daria learned more makeup and hairstyle tips in ten minutes than she had in all of her high school and college years combined. Not that she paid much attention to fashion. She started to tell them about when her sister had the brilliant idea to use a Sharpie as semipermanent eyeliner when a familiar voice stalled her thoughts.

She turned around, and her stomach did all sorts of loop the loops when she saw Tyler walk in with a couple she assumed were the youth leaders. Engaged in conversation, he stopped midsentence when his gaze locked on hers. For a moment that probably felt much longer than it was, he simply stared back at her, the edges of his mouth twitching toward a smile. He said something to his friend, who glanced her way, and the two walked toward her.

Tyler wore dark jeans, his signature cowboy hat, and a green short-sleeved shirt that brightened his eyes and highlighted his muscular physique. He greeted her and Lucy with a polite, "Ma'am," and a tip of his hat.

"I'll be." Lucy's eyes widened. "Tyler Reyes, you've plumb grown up."

He chuckled and slid a hand in his pocket. "Guess so."

"How long's it been? Twenty years?"

"Can't rightly say, ma'am."

"You probably don't remember me, do you?"

His gaze flicked to Daria and lingered before sliding back to Lucy. "Second grade Sunday school."

"I think it was third. Back when we had flannel boards and boom boxes." She laughed and turned to

Drake. "I was hoping to run into you." She vaguely explained Daria's babysitting dilemma.

Drake listened, nodding occasionally. "I can send out a group text and let you know if I get any bites."

Daria smiled. "I appreciate that. Thanks."

"What age?"

She hadn't thought about that. It'd be nice if they had their license in case of an emergency. But she wasn't sure how she felt about having a teenager drive the kids around. "Probably thirteen and older?" She knew a lot of kids started babysitting earlier than that, but this whole parenting thing still felt so new, and that was making her a bit protective.

"All right." Drake high-fived a couple of students as they passed. "On another note, Tyler and I were just talking about your ATV business and the possibility of having a student event out there for some riding and archery. Maybe a bonfire."

She blinked, touched that Tyler had taken the time to help her. Then again, that seemed to be his nature, and from her experience, it was the Sage Creek way. Lucy's raving about this town had proven true. The people in this community looked out for one another. This was the perfect place to raise kids.

She toyed with her bracelet. "I'd love to have the youth group out for riding. However, I don't have an archery range yet." Nor was she certain she would create one.

Tyler gave a one-shoulder shrug. "Won't take long to set up."

Drake greeted a handful of teenage girls as they streamed in one after another and then turned back to Daria. "You know, you might want to check with Elias from Calvary Ranch. He might be interested in bringing a group of kids out."

She nodded. "I've reached out to him a few times, but it won't hurt to follow up." She didn't feel the need to tell him that the group had tentatively scheduled an afternoon to go riding. Meeting the camp director in person, rather than connecting through a cold call, would probably be more effective in motivating him to actually come out.

"He's hard to connect with by phone." Drake grabbed a handful of chips from a nearby dish. "Your best bet is to corner him in person."

She knew entrepreneurs needed to be assertive. She had finally resigned herself to making cold calls, although she still hated it and became tongue-tied with nearly every conversation. The thought of showing up at someone's business uninvited twisted her already jittery stomach.

Her discomfort must have shown, because Lucy quickly interjected. "Tyler, do you know Elias very well?"

"Some."

"Maybe you can introduce him and Daria." She gave Daria's hand a squeeze, as if to offer encouragement.

Honestly, she needed it. Everything was beginning to feel like a steep uphill climb. Considering she viewed herself as fiercely optimistic, her recent discouragement verified her need for a good night's sleep and a day lounging on the couch, two luxuries that seemed out of reach lately.

Tyler's gaze latched onto hers long enough for her cheeks to grow warm. "Sure. I can drive you up there, no problem. It's only about twenty minutes away." He grabbed some oatmeal raisin cookies from a platter. "Hungry?"

She shook her head. "Lucy filled me and the kids up on a month's worth of carbs before we left."

Tyler chuckled. "Sounds like my kind of morning."

"Your mom told me food is your love language." She

clamped her mouth shut, the heat that had already settled into her face rising a few notches. He probably thought she and Ann had sat around talking about him all day, as if Ann were giving Daria tips on how to snag her son or something. Of course, the woman had thrown out some hints, all of which Daria had ignored.

Drake laughed. "That sounds about right." He gazed toward the living room, where most of the students had gathered. He clamped a hand on Tyler's shoulder. "I best get in there before the kids go rogue." He looked at Daria. "I'll call later this week to set something up."

"Thank you."

After he left, Lucy led the three of them back outside and across the lawn toward the church. During the short time they'd been inside, the parking lot had filled to near capacity with a variety of vehicles, some new and shiny, others dented and with peeling paint. Voices merged with the organ's rich notes as families with young children and older couples holding hands made their way up the walk. Two boys, one maybe six, the other nine, chased one another on the lawn until their father called them back. Shoulders slumped, with frowns equal to those Daria had seen on Nolan numerous times, the children complied.

"Reminds me of someone else at that age." Lucy tugged on Tyler's sleeve.

"Come on, now." The mirth in his eyes belied his wounded expression. "I never gave my mama one lick of trouble on Sunday mornings." He winked at Daria, sending her stomach into more acrobatics.

"Right." Lucy gave an exaggerated nod. "Don't believe a word he says."

She laughed. "Oh, I've heard stories." Ann certainly loved to talk about her sons. Daria had always viewed her narrative as the embellished stories of a proud mom. But then Tyler had come and fixed her vehicle, spent a morning surveying her property in the hot June sun, and devoted the rest of his time to helping his mom save the farm. Not to mention he'd initiated that conversation with Drake. "Seriously, though, thanks for opening a door for me with the church youth group. That was a great idea."

"My mom thought of it. She asked if I'd connect you two."

She frowned. Why did his reply leave her disappointed? Hadn't she figured as much? The fact that she hoped his behavior stemmed from personal interest, as if he thought of her at all, concerned her. "Well, then, thank her for me."

"Figure you can thank her yourself when you come help with the fence."

"About that, I know I'd mentioned possibly coming out tomorrow, but I've got free time today, if that works for you."

"Need me to watch the littles?" Lucy asked.

"Nah." Tyler waved a hand. "Nolan can help, and Princess Isla keeps my mom entertained at the house. I can give him his first riding lesson after."

An entire evening with Tyler Reyes, the one man in all of Sage Creek she could easily fall for. If she let herself, which she had no intention of doing.

He glanced toward a couple of teenage boys goofing around outside the parish house and then turned back to Daria. "Those kids can get pretty rowdy even without ATVs and bows and arrows. You'll want to make sure they fully understand and agree to comply with all your rules."

She frowned. She wasn't sure what stung more, the fact that he still blamed her for the damage to his mom's property or that he didn't trust her to run her business responsibly.

Why did she care so much what he thought of her?

That was a question she was trying hard not to think about.

Tyler arrived home from church to find his brother sitting at the table staring at his phone screen while their mom washed and diced stalks of celery. She hadn't joined him for church and had quickly deflected his question when he'd asked her why. The fact that no one had asked him where she was suggested she might not have gone in a while. That didn't seem like her. His dad had always been the reluctant one, wanting to spend his "few free hours" relaxing in front of the television. Was this morning unusual, or had his father's habits eventually become hers?

If so, what else had she withdrawn from? Was Daria now her only friend? The idea that she may have distanced herself from her usual source of support worried him. But that also meant there wasn't much, other than the farm, holding her here. No doubt that would make her moving with him to Omaha less painful. She'd probably grieve the loss of the family farm, but considering her general lack of business sense and the state of the market, she was going to lose it, anyway. It was only a matter of whether he could help her get out from under the situation before this place buried her in insurmountable debt.

His mom must have sensed him watching her, because she glanced back toward where he stood in the kitchen archway and smiled.

"Just in time for lunch." She pulled a golden-brown rotisserie chicken from a Crock-pot and plopped it onto her cutting board.

"Smells good." He deposited his hat onto the table and crossed to the sink.

"Home-baked croissants fresh out of the oven. And I snatched some fresh rhubarb from the garden for tonight's dessert." She motioned with her elbow toward the bowl to her right.

"I've sure missed your home-baked pies."

Her smile wavered slightly. "Guess that's a good reason to stick around, huh?" She took a knife from the rack.

"Meant to mention, Daria's coming by later to help me repair the fence. She's bringing her kids."

"Good. I'll call her and make sure she plans to join us for dinner."

He thought back to the last time they'd spent a meal with them—the tender look on Daria's face whenever she spoke to her children and her soft laugh when they said or did something that amused her.

"Dude."

His brother's voice jolted him back to the present. "What?"

"You're into her."

"Because I'm putting her to work fixing fences?" He scoffed. "If that's your idea of flirting with a woman, you're going to be single a long time, bro."

"Uh-huh." Wesley chuckled. "Who you trying to fool here, me or yourself?"

Their mom cast Wesley a disapproving frown. "That's enough." She shifted her attention to Tyler. "Will you be around this afternoon?"

"If you mean on the property, yes. Although I plan to stop by Michael Hollingworth's. He's giving away a bunch of wooden fence posts, supposedly in good condition." Tyler was trying to save money wherever he could.

"Said he replaced his old stuff with steel. After that, I want to finish cleaning up the pond."

He needed to unclog the overflow pipe to prevent further erosion come the next heavy rain. Based on the tall tangle of brush and dead trees along its bank, no one had tended to that area in some time. Seemed his father had mentally checked out long before leaving physically.

His mom opened a package of walnuts and poured them into a bowl of other chicken-salad ingredients. "As long as you're going to be out and about, would you mind coming with me to Liam's property. He's decided to sell. Says none of his kids want to follow in his footsteps, or the footsteps of their granddaddy, and their granddaddy before that." She shook her head. "Sad to see a legacy lost."

Tyler knew his mom was doing all she could to hold on to her land. Letting go would probably feel like the death of a dream, her entire way of life. But the sooner she grieved what was, the better she'd be able to grab hold of whatever blessings awaited her in Omaha.

"Liam is, what?" Tyler asked. "Going on seventy?"

His mom shrugged. "Something like that."

"Seems a great time to retire."

Her gaze faltered. She took a deep breath and stood a mite straighter. "Anyway, he's selling a bunch of equipment. His old 2013 sprayer with 120 spray booms, a 1,200 gallon tank, and a touch screen display. I was hoping you'd join me to check it out."

No doubt at a cost equivalent to purchasing three new vehicles. "Mom, remember what we talked about?"

She frowned. "I appreciate your concern and listened to your input, but this—" with a sweep of her arm, she indicated the house and likely the property beyond "—is my decision. As I told you before, I'm not selling the family farm."

Wesley's head jerked up. "What?"

Their mom flicked a hand. "Nothing worth worrying about."

In other words, end of conversation. Except he wasn't done. He needed to make sure she didn't go spending money she didn't have.

"Promise me you won't go making any big purchases," he said, hoping his firm tone would ward off any arguments.

She sighed. "Fine. I'll *wait*."

As to her statement regarding this place, unfortunately, she was right. He couldn't force her to sell if she didn't want to, nor could he shield her from any poor financial decisions she chose to make.

He simply needed to help her understand. The best thing he could do in the meantime was tackle the most urgent repairs, clean up the areas most run-down, and pray. He took solace in knowing that God had the power to change hearts and loved his mom even more than he did.

Over lunch, she shifted the conversation to safe topics, such as next month's Fourth of July picnic and parade and who they thought might create the winning float. Meal finished, Tyler helped clean up, despite her protests. Then he filled a large sports bottle with lemonade and headed outside to tackle as much as possible before supper.

With Daria and the kids.

A woman he soon wouldn't see ever again, a fact he'd do well to remember.

Shifting his thoughts to his growing task list, he loaded his machete and chainsaw into the farm truck, an old beater that had been around for as long as he could remember. On the way to the pond, he stopped by the wheat fields to check if the hot afternoon wind had dried them out any. They were close. Since his weather app wasn't predicting rain in the near future, he figured he could start harvesting come Tuesday morning.

Thankfully, he'd found a crew looking for extra acres. He climbed back into the pickup and began making calls, first to the harvesters he'd connected with previously, then with a handful of high school students he knew were looking to earn some extra cash. With people lined up for Tuesday, he followed the curve of the dirt road to the pond he hoped would attract potential buyers if spruced up.

By five o'clock, he'd cut off a section of broken PVC blocking water flow and had created a sizable burn pile from the tangle of brush and dead trees blocking the view of the pond from the house.

There was a good chance whoever bought his mom's place would be homesteaders rather than farmers, looking for a peaceful, picturesque place to raise a family. The pond could be a great selling feature, so could the option to rent acreage to another farmer. Tyler had heard that Uncle Jed was wanting to expand his crops. If true, he'd pay a fair rate to use land so close to his.

Grabbing his tools, Tyler hurried back to the house for a quick shower before supper.

He was heading to the kitchen to help his mom when he heard a vehicle outside. He glanced through the window to see Daria park her car and step out. She'd traded the lavender sundress she'd worn to church for boots, jeans, and a pink T-shirt that complemented her peachy complexion.

Retrieving his hat from the accent table in the foyer, he exited the house and waited on the porch to greet her.

Nolan bolted from the car carrying a plastic dinosaur

in one hand and a toy shovel in the other. "Aunt Daria said I can help." He wore a dress-up carpenter's belt with tools like those in the preschool class at church.

Tyler suppressed an amused chuckle. "I was hoping you would. You came well prepared, I see."

Little man grinned and bobbed his head. "Can we ride horses now?"

"Nolan, remember what I told you when we were driving over?" Daria helped Isla from her car seat and then went around to the trunk of her car.

The child gave a loud sigh. "We're here to work." He slumped his shoulders so dramatically, Tyler couldn't help but laugh.

He quickly covered with a cough. "That's right. A man's got to take care of business first." He tossed Daria a wink, igniting the most endearing blush upon her cheeks. He quickly shifted his focus back onto Nolan. "But don't worry, there'll be plenty of time for riding."

"Yay!" Nolan jumped up and down.

Isla copied, raising her chubby fisted hands in the air.

The joy radiating from Daria's deep brown eyes as she watched the children captivated him. A gentle wind stirred wisps of her hair, streaked with wine-toned highlights that had escaped from her ponytail. A few strands got stuck in her long, dark lashes, and he felt a sudden urge to brush them away. Instead, he shoved a hand in his pocket and jiggled his spare change.

"There are my favorite grasshoppers." His mom pushed through the screen door, letting it bang closed behind her, and dropped to one knee, arms open. "Come and give Nana Ann some sugar."

As if owning the nickname, Nolan hopped up the stairs, pawing the air and flicking his tongue in and out.

Head tilted, Isla stared at him for a moment. Then, clutching the railing, she scampered onto the porch.

Smiling wider than Tyler had seen all day, his mom swept them into one of the hugs he remembered well from his childhood days. Her hugs, the almond-cherry scent of her lotion, and her baked goods always made this place feel like home.

With Isla on her hip, she struggled to her feet. She eyed Nolan's tool belt. "You look official."

Nolan frowned. "What's that?"

Now standing beside him, Daria smoothed his bangs from his forehead. "Like a carpenter."

The crevice between his brows deepened. Arms crossed, he shook his head. "No. Farmer. Like Mr. Tyler."

The child's obvious admiration evoked Tyler's longing for a family. One day, he'd have a little guy with cheeky smiles, bright eyes, and more questions than a man could answer following him around. And a smart, witty, and beautiful woman to share his meals and his dreams with.

"Tell you what." His mom gave Isla's chubby knee a squeeze, initiating a high-pitched squeal. "Y'all do whatever you need to while Isla and I stay in the nice air-conditioned house and make us all something sweet for after supper."

Tyler's mouth watered at the thought of her homemade rhubarb pie, hot and gooey with a crunchy brown-sugar topping, fresh out of the oven. "Now that sounds like a plan."

"Where's Cookie?" Nolan glanced about.

Tyler's mom planted a hand on her hip. "Well, now. I don't rightly know. Probably staying out of the sun somewhere."

"Can we go find her?" Nolan asked.

His mom looked at Daria.

She shrugged. "If Nana Ann's okay taking you and it won't mess with her plans."

His mom's smile widened as if she'd just learned she'd won a kitchen remodel. "What plans?" She descended the steps and, with Isla still on her hip, took Nolan's hand in hers. "Don't worry about us none. We won't get into too much trouble, will we, darlin'?" Glancing down at the little man, she swung his arm.

The child giggled and shook his head.

Tyler's mom appeared to have caught the Nana bug. God willing, he'd give her grandkids of her own soon enough. At least two—a boy and a girl.

Chapter Six

Daria watched Ann and the kids stroll down the gravel road toward the chicken coop, pigpen, and the hay barn. She'd come to Sage Creek looking for support and had found a dear friend and two doting "grandmas" in the process.

"You ready?"

She turned at the sound of Tyler's deep voice. "Absolutely."

"Vehicle's this way." He hooked a thumb toward a rusted blue pickup with peeling paint and a wooden bed carrying what looked like old fence posts and an assortment of tools.

Neither of them spoke as she fell into step beside him. She should probably initiate conversation, but about what? Talking about the weather, or whatever his mom had planned for supper, felt cliché.

He beat her to the truck and opened her door for her, his strong biceps straining against the sleeve of his T-shirt. His eyes latched onto hers, spiking her pulse.

Face warm, she ducked under his arm and into the cab, acutely aware of his nearness. "Thank you." Averting her gaze, she occupied herself with her seat belt.

He gave one quick nod, rounded the truck, and hopped in, his leathery-citrus scent wafting toward her. He turned the key in the ignition. With a glance in the rearview mirror, he shifted to Reverse and backed out. They bounced along the heavily potholed road leading to the far side of Ann's property, and once again, she searched for something to say.

Their silence felt comfortable, though.

Five minutes later, he tapped his brakes as a doe, one shade darker than the wheat tufts, pranced across the road. Her speckled fawn followed close behind.

She'd never tire of seeing God's creatures roam freely. "That's one of the things I love about Sage Creek."

"The deer?"

"Animals—and nature—in general. It feels so...peaceful." Much different than the city's clogged sidewalks and busy highways where everyone always seems in such a hurry. "It must have been nice growing up in a place like this."

"It had its pluses."

"But?"

"Just wasn't what I wanted, I guess."

That was likely why he was so bent on moving to Omaha, and it was a significant reason she and Tyler were incompatible. It seemed he wanted to get away from the type of life she felt increasingly drawn to.

But would he leave Ann to run the farm alone?

"I can tell your mom's grateful to have you here." She knew Ann was worried about the delayed harvest. Tyler's presence had to ease her anxiety. Make her feel less alone.

A tendon in his jaw twitched. "Probably should've come around more."

"I'm sure it was hard being in the military and all."

He rubbed the back of his neck. "Guess I didn't realize how bad things had gotten."

Did he mean with the farm or his parents' marriage? "You talk to your dad much?"

"An email now and again."

His expression suggested this wasn't a topic he wanted to discuss, not that she blamed him. Although she hadn't heard the full story, she knew how much Ann had struggled over the past six months that she'd known her.

"What about you?" He cast her a sideways glance. "You always live in the city?"

She never knew how much to share in response to these types of questions. She certainly didn't want to say anything that might trigger further conversation about that time period. Frankly, she tried not to think about it. Seemed maybe she and Tyler had something in common.

"Pretty much." Gazing out her side window, she watched cotton-ball clouds drift across the pale blue sky.

He stopped at the end of the fence line. A sizable strawberry patch with bright red berries poking through thickly clustered leaves stretched diagonal to the corner post. Here, her trail merged with Ann's dirt road and bordered her field before cutting through county land to the lake. A golden hawk glided above them, close enough she could make out the banding on his tail and the streaks of brown coloring his cream feathers.

Tyler's phone chimed. He read the text and then made eye contact. "You're off tomorrow, right?"

She nodded and followed him to his pickup bed to help unload, grasshoppers springing out of their way as they walked.

Tyler handed her a rusted post puller and then hoisted two posts that appeared used onto his shoulder. "I reached out to the fella who directs the Christian camp we talked about this morning. Asked if we could come out. He's free tomorrow, if that works for you."

We? As in go together? In one vehicle, just the two of them? The idea caused her pulse to stutter.

She covered her rogue reaction with what she hoped appeared a confident smile. "That'd be wonderful. Thank you."

Lucy had encouraged her to increase her networking skills. Despite her introverted nature, Daria was trying. She'd joined the local chamber of commerce, a rural entrepreneurs' group, paid dues to a women-in-business organization, and had even visited with some boys' club leaders. But she always felt like an outside peddler. Knowing unhealed wounds from her time in foster care likely tainted her perspective didn't alleviate her anxiety regarding what felt to her like spamming strangers.

Regardless, Tyler could act as an endorsement.

But what about the children? "So long as I can find someone to watch Nolan and Isla. Lucy works until four or five."

"You hear back from Drake?"

"He gave me some names and numbers, but I haven't had a chance to interview anyone."

"He wouldn't recommend anyone that's not high quality and trustworthy. 'Course, if you'd feel more comfortable, the sitter can always watch the kids here under my mom's eye."

Inviting someone to Ann's felt intrusive. "I'd hate to put her out."

"You kidding? It'd make her day. Have you noticed how she lights up when y'all come over?"

Daria laughed. "She does seem to enjoy children."

"Guess it's her inner grandmother shining through. Probably figures, since my brother and I haven't given her any rug rats to spoil, she's got to go out and gather some herself."

Did Tyler want children? He'd make a great father. And husband.

He retrieved the remaining tools and a bucket, which he placed near their feet, and then straightened. The crevice between his thick brows suggested something bothered him. "When did my mom last go to church?"

"Honestly? I think she's only gone once since I've been here. But I don't think you need to be worried about her spiritually." Not anymore, anyway.

"What then?"

She didn't want to betray her friend's confidence, especially since she didn't have anything concrete to go on. But she also knew Tyler asked from genuine concern. Maybe if he realized how difficult the past year had been for his mom, he wouldn't be in such a rush to leave.

But how much of her desire to see him stay stemmed from her concern for Ann versus her desire to get to know him better?

What a ridiculous question. Of course, her love for her friend motivated her, not the cowboy's rugged good looks, kind disposition, and loyal nature. Or the way Nolan and Isla both seemed completely smitten with the man.

Daria would be wise to limit their time with Tyler. She and the kids didn't need another hard goodbye, and that was the only way their interactions with him would end.

"Daria?"

She released a breath. "She never said anything specific, but when we first met, I sensed she was mad at God."

"Because my dad left?"

She nodded.

"And now?"

"I think she's worried people are judging her."

He scrubbed a hand over his face and nodded. "Makes sense. Sometimes the greatest blessings living in small towns can also be a downfall."

"Everyone knows everyone and their business?"

"Right." He turned toward the broken fence post and gave it a kick. "The wood here's in poor shape. Doubt those college kids would've made a dent otherwise. Some might even say they did me a favor in forcing me to repair something that's been neglected too long."

She smiled. "Glad to help." True or not, she still felt bad about the damage, especially with all the work Ann and her boys had ahead. If this section was indicative of all their fencing, they had quite a project to tackle.

He handed her his wire cutters. "See this mess wrapped around the stake?"

"Yeah?"

"You'll want to cut here." He pointed. "And here."

She appreciated his step-by-step instructions on something that could prove useful on her property, if not at the rental, then when she had her own plot of land.

"Field and Ammo is having a sale on archery targets." She lifted her hair off her neck, letting the gentle breeze cool her. "They didn't seem too expensive." At least, not compared to building a motocross course.

He dropped a barbed staple into his bucket. "You can probably make them yourself. Some folks use hay bales, which is probably your easiest option, although they tend to fall apart in the rain."

"Are you a hunter?"

"Not much anymore, but some buddies and I got into it in high school. We started it as a way to control feral hogs that were destroying our farm."

"I read about that. The article said they create over

200 million dollars' worth of damages in Texas alone. Each year."

"They've been out of control for a while."

"Did you shoot any?"

"Some. We would have done a whole lot better if we'd used rifles, but we were too cocky for that. Wanted to prove ourselves, to who, I have no idea." He chuckled. "Except maybe ourselves."

Scratching his jaw, he stared into the distance. "You know, you might be able to work something out with the local farmers. Tourist hunting. You provide the bows, maybe even hire someone to school folks on how to use 'em."

That wasn't a bad idea, except she wasn't sure how her neighbors felt about her. They were nice and all, but she got the sense they were leery of her, Tyler's "uncle" Jed especially. She'd seen him nosing about near the edge of her property more than once. Although he never actually did anything, his behavior made her feel...scrutinized.

Lucy would probably say Daria's perception was tainted with an underlying fear of rejection related to her childhood. That could be true. Daria had come a long way from her wounded teenage days, but she still had a lot of hurts to process.

She and Tyler spent the rest of the time talking about everything from escaping bulls to crop-destroying hailstorms. By the time they arrived back at the house, thick cloud cover had moved in, dropping the temperature nearly twenty degrees. Ann and the children were on the porch, Ann gently swaying in the benched swing while Isla finger painted, and Nolan loaded pebbles into an old wooden dump truck.

Tyler watched Nolan play. "Nana Ann's got you working I see."

He shook his head. "This is just pretend."

Tyler chuckled. "Ah. Right." He tossed Daria a wink. Cheeks ignited, she quickly averted her gaze.

Nolan turned toward her. "Can I make a worm farm?"

"A what?"

"A worm farm, to sell to fisherman and stuff. Like Mr. Tyler did when he was my age."

Tyler shot his mom an amused look. "You told him about that, did you?"

Ann laughed. "Of course. I've divulged all your secrets, haven't I, munchkin?" She nudged Nolan.

He nodded, gaze on Daria. "Can I, Auntie? I won't make a mess, and it won't cost nothing."

She loved seeing her nephew's enthusiasm. "I don't know why not."

"Yay!" Grinning, he sprang to his feet. "Mr. Tyler, can you help me find 'em? Uncuz I don't know where they live."

Mirth filled his eyes. "Only if you'll share the proceeds."

Nolan's frown indicated he wasn't sure how he felt about that.

"Don't worry, little man." Tyler gave him a gentle nudge. "I'm just joshin'."

The boy's face brightened once again. "I can give you some of my slushie. From the Gas-n-Go."

"Well, now." Tyler raised an eyebrow. "I can't refuse an offer like that."

His gentle banter touched Daria. This farm was good for Nolan—healing—and Tyler clearly had a way with children.

Too bad he didn't plan to stay.

Sitting on the porch beside Nolan, Tyler pushed around a stone, making honking noises whenever his make-believe vehicle bumped into the dump truck or the boy's shin. Nolan giggled and scooted back.

He sure was a cute kid. If Tyler stuck around long enough, he could easily become attached to both munchkins.

And their beautiful aunt.

He cast Daria a sideways glance, captivated by the tenderness in her eyes as she engaged with her niece. It couldn't have been easy stepping into a parenting role so unexpectedly, all while still grieving her sister.

Daria surveyed Isla's artwork. "This is how childhood should be—peaceful, with opportunities to explore, play in the dirt, and engage in creative activities."

Ann lifted a glass of iced sweet tea. "Y'all get fixed what needed fixing?"

Tyler nodded. "The section we set out to, yeah."

"I hear you, son. Seems there's always something to repair. Bit by bit, right?"

He glanced at the section of gravel where his brother normally parked. "Where's Wesley?"

His mom smiled. "Out on a date."

He raised his eyebrows. "With who?"

She shrugged. "He's been tight-lipped about this one, but I get the feeling it's serious. At least to Wesley."

Interesting. Maybe the woman would motivate him to grow up.

"Y'all hungry?" His mom stood. "It's about suppertime."

Daria sprang to her feet. "How can I help?"

"Y'all just relax." She flicked a hand. "And get to discussing that worm farm before the fishermen come looking."

"Smart thinking." Tyler turned to Nolan. "What kind of container do you think you'll need to raise worms in?"

The boy tilted his head. "One that holds dirt."

Laugh lines framed Tyler's eyes. "That seems important." He handed Nolan chalk and some paper Isla had yet to saturate with paint. "Want to draw a sketch?"

"Then horse riding?"

"Absolutely."

By the time his mom called them in, Nolan had asked about every possible question related to worms, fish, and horses and had shared an encyclopedia worth of dinosaur facts. Isla toddled after his mom, stopped at the door, and then turned back around. Big brown eyes on his, she slipped her chubby, paint-stained hand in his. Warmth swept through him. Tyler could get used to evenings like this.

Except that he'd be leaving soon.

Maybe if he reminded himself of that often enough, he could walk away from this sweet little family with his heart intact. Regardless, he couldn't stay, not without forfeiting the well-paying job his buddy had helped him get. His friend had put his reputation on the line to vouch for him.

Entering the kitchen, he shifted his thoughts to the much safer territory of grain markets and the latest weather predictions. According to his app, they were in for higher than normal temperatures for the next few days. For once, he was pleased to see that.

With all the help he'd lined up, they might get their crop harvested in time for his mom to earn enough of a profit that she could walk away debt free.

His brother returned as their mom was pulling her famous fresh-baked rolls from the oven. "Smells amazing." He sat in their father's old position at the head of the table, across from their mom, and guzzled half a glass of sweet tea. "I'm famished."

His mom set out three types of dressing. "I thought you had someplace to be?"

"Earlier, yah." He quickly transitioned to something he'd read on crop diversification. "I heard the price for cotton's expected to increase next year."

"I agree with your logic." His mom dabbed her mouth with her napkin. "I'd like us to add that and soybeans."

Wesley nodded. "I can help create realistic yield goals and set up a seeding plan. That way you can take advantage of the early buy rates."

"We've got time." She stabbed a cucumber slice with her fork. "But yes, that would be helpful."

Tyler suppressed a sigh. It was hard enough convincing his mom to sell this place without his brother feeding her false hope, which was precisely what he was doing. Wesley simply didn't have the gumption or drive to keep this place afloat, and it was too heavy of a load for their mom to carry alone. Not to mention, neither she nor Wesley had much business sense. That had always been his father's area, and he doubted she had the funds to hire a farm manager.

Taking a swig of his drink, Wesley looked at Daria. "Were you able to get Nolan registered for flag football?"

"I left a message with some questions regarding the age cutoff, but I haven't heard back."

"Let me know if you need me to reach out to my buddy at the parks department," his brother said.

She smiled. "Thank you."

Why did the fact that his brother knew something about Daria that Tyler didn't cause his shoulders to clench? This wasn't middle school, nor did he have any claims on the woman. If anything, his brother had more of a right to such information, since he apparently planned to remain in Sage Creek.

The notion didn't make him feel better, and not just because she and the kids deserved a hardworking man.

He crumpled his napkin and tossed it onto his plate. "That was delicious, as usual."

His mom beamed. "It's nice having a full table to cook for once again."

Tyler thought of all the meals he'd spent in this space, most of them pleasant. The after-school snacks he'd come home to and fluffy blueberry pancakes and thick slabs of bacon each Saturday morning. All the late-night conversations between him and his mom when something he'd been fretting about kept him up. The times she'd reached across the table to cover his hand with hers and pray.

Somehow, she always sensed when he needed her. He'd creep downstairs and into the kitchen in search of something sweet, knowing she'd soon appear in her floral nightgown and slippers. She'd place some cookies between them and then wait patiently until he felt ready to talk. There'd been no prodding or pestering when he wasn't up to sharing.

Daria stood with her plate.

His mom stopped her midway to the sink. "Wesley and I can manage cleanup. Y'all better take the munchkins to see the horses before this little one about jumps out of his skin."

Daria laughed. "He can wait, I assure you."

"Oh, I'm sure he can. But there's no need for that when there are two able-bodied adults ready to do the washing. Besides, Wesley and I have boring business matters to discuss, don't we, son?"

"Yep." Wesley made a shooing motion.

What business matters? Wesley was about the last person their mom should listen to in that regard.

Tyler eyed his mom and brother. He was looking forward to spending time with Daria and her little ones, perhaps too much so. But he wasn't thrilled with knowing his brother would probably be feeding their mom ideas that would only raise her hopes and end in failure.

Tyler brought the dressings and half-empty salad bowl to the counter and then faced Daria. "Ready?"

"I am." She hoisted Isla onto her hip, following Nolan as he lunged, hopped, and skipped to the door.

Once outside, Nolan darted ahead, and Tyler fell in step beside Daria. "Would love to bottle me up some of that boy's energy."

She regarded him with furrowed brow. "If you're tired, we don't have—"

"Nah, I'm just teasing." He spoke too quickly, seemed too eager. "A relaxing evening with the horses will do me good." Time with Daria wouldn't dampen his night, either.

"I really appreciate you doing this."

The admiration in her eyes made him want to please her even more. And that was a dangerous notion.

Nolan reached the gate leading to the east pasture before the rest of them. He scampered up the rails and then hung upside down from his hands and knees. Upon seeing her brother swaying upside down, Isla fussed and pushed against Daria.

"All right, Miss Squirmy Pants." She'd barely placed the child on her feet before the princess toddled toward her brother, quite frustrated at her lack of climbing ability.

"Need help?" Tyler lifted her up so that she stood on the bottom board, then he lifted her to the next rail, almost as if she'd done the climbing herself.

They let the children play for a bit, then Tyler led the way to the stables. He scooped grain from the large plastic barrel outside the tack room and poured some into each child's hands. Ginger, a chestnut quarter horse with a strip of white from muzzle to mane, poked her head over her gate and neighed.

Nolan giggled, jumped up and down, and lurched forward.

Daria grabbed him by the wrist. "Wait for Mr. Tyler's instructions, please."

"Yes, ma'am." Voice flat, he slumped.

Tyler placed a hand on the boy's shoulder. "It's hard being patient, isn't it, little man?"

Nolan nodded, gaze locked on Ginger.

"When you feed a horse, you want to keep your hand flat, like this." He demonstrated with half a handful of grain. "Otherwise, she might accidentally nip your fingers." He tickled the boy's ribs, eliciting a snicker.

"Me pwease! Me pwease!" Princess wriggled to get free, only this time, Daria held the girl tightly. The tension in Daria's face suggested she was afraid of horses.

It looked like Tyler had two jobs, to give Nolan some beginning riding lessons while also alleviating his aunt's fear.

Fifteen minutes later, he'd cinched on the child's saddle he'd unburied from the junk barn and was slowly leading Nolan and Ginger around the corral. At first, Daria watched with a tight expression, almost as if she were holding her breath. A few laps later, she seemed to relax some, although she remained alert.

After about a dozen times around, Nolan began yawning.

Tyler stopped near where Daria stood holding an equally tired Isla. "I'm guessing these two will sleep well tonight?"

Daria smiled. "Looks that way. Again, thank you for this. This evening has been wonderful."

Yes, it had been. So much so, that he was reluctant for it to end.

He lifted Nolan from the saddle, guided him to slip under the fence railing to Daria, and then led Ginger to the stall.

They were waiting for him just outside the stables.

He closed the double doors. "Considering I'll only have a couple weeks to work with him, I think it'll be best if we aim for three nights a week or so. That will at least give him enough time to decide whether or not he wants to continue." Although he'd yet to meet a kid that didn't fall in love with the sport from first ride. "If he does, I can help you find someone to step in once I'm gone."

She dropped her gaze.

Was she worried about the cost? Was it wrong that he wanted to cover that for her? He could certainly afford to do so, especially once he started his railroad job. Besides, riding would be a perfect outlet for the boy. A way to bring joy into his life and maybe lessen the ache of his grief. Seemed only right to help if he could. Wasn't that what Pastor Roger always preached about—finding ways to brighten people's darkness?

He could even give one of their horses to the boy, paying his mom fair value, of course. He'd hoped to sell all but two, which he'd planned on stabling at a ranch outside Omaha.

Would Daria accept the gift? She seemed the independent type. Probably by necessity, with all she'd gone through.

She was strong, determined, resilient, and beautiful. Why hadn't someone snatched her up already?

Someone would soon enough.

He couldn't shake the feeling that he'd be the one missing out.

Chapter Seven

Daria scrutinized her appearance in the mirror with a frown. She glanced at the outfits spread across her bed behind her and then at her near empty closet. *Just pick something already.* She couldn't remember the last time she'd fussed over what to wear like this.

Actually, she could. The day Christopher James had asked her to be his date to roller-skating night in the sixth grade. She and her sister hadn't been living with Lucy for long and were still processing life through the lens of their previous placements. Some of their foster parents had been so critical, breathing itself had practically felt like a rebellion. On the opposite end had been a hippie couple who'd apparently thought children would thrive so long as they had a safe place to sleep and access to food.

Daria had managed well enough, in part because her love for books had helped her form a close relationship with the school librarian. Her sister hadn't responded quite so well. By the time they'd moved in with Lucy, Daria's sister had already begun to self-destruct.

When Lucy took them in, Daria had begun to heal. For the first time ever, she'd felt she might actually have found a place to belong.

That, and not any feelings toward Christopher or any other boy, was what had caused her to fuss over her appearance.

And now?

Now she genuinely cared what Tyler thought of her, and that concerned her.

She released a heavy breath. *Daria Ellis, what are you doing?*

This was not like her, nor was it wise.

Maybe today's outing wasn't such a great idea, not that she could cancel. Not without appearing completely irresponsible. That would definitely keep Calvary Ranch's camp director from doing business with her.

Tyler was offering her an in, one that could potentially lead to steady business nine months out of the year and immeasurable word-of-mouth value.

She thought back to the night before, and how sweet Tyler had been with the kids. Nolan clearly adored him. What wasn't to like? He was kind, gentle yet strong, a man who lived by his convictions.

The admiration that shined in his eyes whenever he glanced Daria's way or listened to her talk only increased her desire to succeed.

That was a good thing, right? To gain strength from those around her, however brief their interactions?

So long as her heart, which seemed to have a mind of its own of late, didn't long for more. At least, not from Tyler Reyes.

With a sigh, she glanced at the time on her phone, fluffed her hair one last time, and headed to the living room. The children were watching cartoons with a handful of toys strewn around them. Nolan wore his dinosaur backpack filled with a plethora of toys and scavenged treasures. Isla stood at the coffee table arranging colorful cereal rings in a line.

Upon seeing Daria, Lucy stood. "Beautiful and professional."

Daria smiled. "Thanks. Being a northerner, I'm never quite sure how to dress." She grabbed a hand-designed leather briefcase Lucy had gifted her with the day she signed the papers for her business, Isla's diaper bag, and a paper sack of the children's favorite snacks. "You kiddos ready?"

Nolan sprang to his feet. "To see Cookie and her puppies and feed the horses and find eggs for Nana Ann."

She frowned. "Remember, Nana Ann has work to do today." Isla on her hip, she led the way out of the house and to the car.

Nolan hurried after her. "Ms. Jessie will play with us?"

"Yes." Hopefully, the teenager Drake had recommended would be able to keep the children from becoming a nuisance.

"But not Mr. Tyler?"

"That is correct." Her stomach tumbled at the mention of his name—a reaction one might expect to lessen the more time she spent with him. If anything, her nervous anticipation only increased the more time they spent together.

Nolan peppered her with questions the entire drive to the Reyeses' property. The tendency she normally found endearing only increased her jitters. As a result, she arrived at Ann's feeling as if she'd guzzled an entire pot of coffee.

She'd barely parked when Tyler stepped out of the house in boots, dark-blue jeans, and a purple T-shirt that accentuated his tan.

"Morning." Descending the porch stairs, he tipped his

hat at her before turning his attention to Nolan. The child had bolted from his booster and stood before him, fighting to unzip his backpack. No doubt to show him one of the half a dozen or so dinosaurs he'd brought. "What do you got there, little man?"

The amusement in his eyes, as if her nephew brought him joy, touched Daria. "Just about every toy, gadget, and pebble the kiddo owns."

Tyler chuckled. "Makes sense. A fella never knows what he might need, right?" He tousled the child's hair and turned to greet Isla, who, always her brother's shadow, began searching her diaper bag's pockets.

Apparently, all she could find was her polka-dotted sippy cup, which she held out. "Mine."

Tyler rested a hand on his belt buckle. "Really?"

Isla nodded and quickly took a drink as if to prove it.

"That looks mighty good. You sure it's not mine?"

Brow furrowed, she shook her head and took half a step back as if afraid he'd take it from her.

The screen door creaked open as Ann exited the house. "Is Mr. Tyler teasing you, sweet pea?" She descended the stairs, scooped the toddler into her arms, and kissed the fat folds on her neck. "Now off you go." She shooed Tyler and Daria.

Daria had intended to wait until her sitter arrived, but Ann was insistent.

They took Tyler's truck, in part because he knew the way, but also to avoid having to transfer the car seat and booster seat. As they were turning onto the country road, Jessie pulled onto the property with a cheerful wave.

Daria exhaled. "I'm glad to see she arrived on time. I worried the children might disrupt your mom's morning."

Tyler lowered his visor as the curve of the road led

them directly into the sun. "You know she loves every minute she spends with those two."

"She's been amazing. Truly."

"Seems you've been good for her as well. Thanks for being here for her when I wasn't." His tone carried a note of sorrow, or maybe regret.

"You're here now. That's what matters."

They drove in silence for a bit, the hum of the engine disrupted by the occasional clunk of their tires crossing cracks in the road. Outside her window, golden wheat fields blurred into pasturelands dotted with vibrant wildflowers and an occasional farmhouse. Ahead of them, a tractor came into view, followed by a sparsely populated herd of longhorns.

At a three-way stop, he continued onto a gravel road through a thickening expanse of trees and across a wooden bridge. Water flowed around large boulders below them, and a handful of tents poked out from the cluster of green beyond.

She checked her phone. "What's the reception like out here?"

"Hit and miss." Tyler drove past a row of cabins, each maybe five hundred square feet in size. "But my mom can always call the office phone if she needs to get ahold of you."

She rubbed her collarbone. "I was actually thinking about the guy I've got working for me. He's new and doesn't seem that comfortable making decisions. Not that I expect he'll need to. But this is all new territory for me." Every area of her life was actually. Parenting, owning a business, being a boss.

He pulled into a large dirt lot in front of a wooden lodge and cut the engine. "What's his name? Maybe I know him."

Considering everyone in Sage Creek knew everyone else, she imagined he did. "Jason Youtz. He's the son of one of Lucy's friends."

"Doesn't sound familiar. When did he graduate?"

"This past May."

Tyler paused mid-reach for the door and turned back toward her with a frown. "How often does he work for you?"

He looked concerned, almost as if he worried the guy might take advantage of her or something. It wasn't like she kept cash lying around her office or had any to keep lying around.

She shrugged. "He pretty much comes in on an as-needed basis. He's got a job working at the Grain and Feed. The ATV job is just his side gig. I don't mind adjusting his schedule, and he doesn't mind the low hours I give him. So it works."

Her answer didn't appear to ease his mind.

Did he doubt her competency as an employer? Her ability to hire and manage capable staff? She was probably just being overly sensitive.

The bigger question, however, was why was his opinion of her so important?

She knew better than to give a man this much sway over her emotions, especially one who already had one boot out of town.

Tyler paused on the curb to shake some sense into his overprotective brain. There was no reason a guy fresh out of high school couldn't man Off Roadin' It for a few hours in Daria's absence. Even if he'd been the one to rent to those rowdy college boys—something Tyler wasn't sure of—it wasn't any of his business. None of it was except for when Daria's endeavors affected his mom's livelihood.

He probably wouldn't be so worried if not for an incident that had occurred back when he was in high school. Some kids tearing through his parents' newly planted fields had cost his family thousands of dollars' worth of lost crops, and their fields weren't the only ones hit. The cops had never caught the hoodlums, and that hadn't been the last time someone's crops had been torn up. Seemed there was always a group of kids ready to make someone else's land their personal playground.

Looking back on that summer, he could now see that his dad's poor planning had led to their greatest financial struggles. But his dad, too proud to admit his mistakes, had made those boys a scapegoat. He'd said they were the reason he couldn't match Tyler's savings toward his first car as he'd promised.

In a way, that's what the farm represented to him, promises broken and blame shifted. That and his dad always expecting him and his brother to work doubly hard for extra-long to make up for his mess-ups. Mistakes Tyler wouldn't have minded so much if only his father had owned up to them instead of blaming everyone else.

None of any of that was Daria's fault or worth putting a damper on their day.

He inhaled the scent of sunbaked earth, wood chips, and decaying leaf litter. "Man, does this bring back memories. I spent many a night right here at this camp." He opened the door for her and followed her inside as the bell above their heads chimed.

"I always wanted to go to summer camp."

"You never went to camp?" a male voice said.

Tyler turned, nodding hello as Elias rose from his desk to greet them.

The men shook hands. "Thank you for meeting with us." Tyler introduced Daria and the camp director to one another.

"Good morning." Daria's tight smile revealed nervousness.

Tyler felt an urge to encourage her in some way. He got the impression making a sales call, as this technically was, made her uncomfortable. Yet here she was, courageously stepping out with an endearing blend of determination and vulnerability.

Elias widened his stance. "What was that I heard when y'all walked in? Is it true you never went to summer camp?"

"Correct." Although her tone conveyed confidence, she began fiddling with her bracelet, a nervous tell Tyler had picked up on. "I can't say that I've had that pleasure."

"Guess we best give you a bit of the experience while you're here. What do you say?"

She smiled. "I appreciate you sharing your time with us."

"My pleasure." He led the way out and to a trailhead in the wooded area behind a two-story hotel-like structure. "As you may have seen when you came in, we have single and double bedroom cabins, two lodges down yonder, one that sleeps twelve, another twenty-four, along with one unit of apartments. A lot of families rent those. Minimum stay's three days. Most folks come for a week."

Daria and Tyler followed behind Elias over the rocky terrain. The sun filtered through the trees, dotting the path with light. A bullfrog croaked in the distance, and a squirrel scampered across the path, over a boulder and a fallen and rotting log, before disappearing into the brush.

Daria ducked beneath a low-lying branch. "Are most of your campers kids?"

"About seventy percent." Elias stepped over a tangle of exposed weeds. "We've hosted everything from retreats for men, women, writers' groups, and carving organizations to youth camps and family reunions."

Tyler slapped at a mosquito on his arm. "Nice. You're open spring, summer, and fall?"

"We're actually talking about staying open year-round and maybe even doing some sort of Christmas light display, like you might see in a big city zoo."

The sound of laughter and conversation drifted toward them. "Up here is our challenge course," Elias said as they turned a corner.

They stopped in an open area that had rope, some single, others webbed, stretched between the tall trees. Teens in red helmets stood at the top of one of Tyler's favorite structures as a kid—the zip line. Diagonal from this, maybe fifty feet in the air, half a dozen harnessed students paired together were making their way across one of the challenge courses. The "steps" were floating planks, about half of them far enough apart that they needed another's help to reach them.

"I never did so hot on that exercise." He pointed. "I was too bullheaded and impatient. Always tried to force my partner to go faster but only ended up knocking us both off balance."

"Your leader make you start over?"

He chuckled. "Oh, yeah. Probably climbed more stairs that day than a fireman in training."

"Sounds like that's where you two should start then." Grinning, Elias turned to Daria. "What do you say? Think you and Tyler here could take on some of our middle schoolers? See who can make it across first?"

Her wide-eyed stare ignited Tyler's protective side. Poor woman looked terrified. He hooked a thumb in his belt loop and scratched his jaw. "I don't know about that. We don't want to take up too much of your time."

"Nonsense. It'd be my pleasure." He looked at Daria. "Matter of fact, knowing you had your first camp experience here, a smidgeon of it, anyway, would about make my year."

Elias was adamant and enthusiastic. How could Tyler decline without offending the guy? Then again, this was a great opportunity for Daria. It'd give her a sense of accomplishment.

Plus, she'd be reliant on him. Completely focused on him. Hand in hand, eye to eye, him lending her his strength, and her letting him.

Careful, Tyler. You're treading on dangerous ground, buddy.

He'd come to Sage Creek to help his mom salvage whatever assets she had left, not to fall for a beautiful woman determined to sink roots in the place he was so set to leave.

"All right then." Elias gave a single clap. "Let's get you both suited up."

Tyler and Daria followed the director to a pile of equipment on a tarp near a thick-trunked tree. He watched her closely as Elias helped her into her harness. Was she frightened or focused? Probably a bit of both, considering she'd never done anything like this before. But he'd been around her enough to know she wouldn't want him to make a fuss. Especially not in front of a prospective client.

Once geared up, Elias handed them helmets and led them to the base of the balance apparatus.

"Ladies first." Tyler motioned toward the stairs and then followed her up.

When she'd ascended a third of the way, she stopped and glanced down.

"You okay?" Tyler asked.

She took in a visible breath and shot him a smile that didn't reach her anxious eyes. "Yep. Just catching my breath."

"You've got this."

She cast him a wobbly glance and then eyed their middle-school competitors climbing the stairs across the way. "For team adults, right?" She gave him a fist bump.

He grinned. "You know it."

The lady had grit. She was obviously nervous, but it was also clear that she had no intention of giving in.

A man could build a life with a woman like that. Too bad their paths were heading in opposite directions.

A staffer wearing a yellow helmet and matching vest waited for them at the top. He flashed Daria a smile. "You good?"

She gripped the side railing, her knees slightly bent, almost as if she wanted to sit down. Or maybe she was worried the boards beneath her might give way.

"Ready." She stepped closer to the right side of the podium and waited while the man connected her with the cable above them using lobster claws.

"This will keep you secure even if your feet slip." He gave the rope a hard tug to verify its strength.

Her face blanched.

"Don't worry." Tyler locked eyes with her. "I won't let you fall."

"No man left behind?"

"Or woman." He winked. "I'll go first." He stepped onto the first platform and then turned and extended his hand.

She stared at it for a moment and then reached for

him. Stretching his arm, he gripped her hand firmly and gently. Then, careful to follow her pace, he led her forward and onto his plank.

Her face lit up.

He laughed. "Bam."

As they progressed, her movements became surer and her smiles more frequent.

And her soft hand was a perfect fit in his.

The distance between the planks increased enough as they neared the end so that she would need to lunge to make it to the finish. The board beneath her swayed. Legs visibly trembling, she clutched the thick metal cords attaching the plank to the line above her.

"Last one." He extended his hand, knowing the distance between them probably felt inconceivably wide but also knowing that it was within her reach. First, however, she'd have to release her stranglehold and commit. A timid step wouldn't cut it. "You've got this."

She gave a weak nod, but her feet remained planted.

He'd talked a soldier buddy out of a panic attack a time or two. Often, a person just needed to focus on their strength and to replace what-if scenarios with truth. "Remember what Elias said when you were stepping into your harness? About what happens if you slip?"

"I'll dangle in the air." Her wobbly voice suggested she didn't find that comforting.

"That's right. Safe and secure. Like you were sitting in one of those swing rides at the county fair, only ten times as strong. How much weight did Elias say your gear could hold?"

"Five thousand pounds?"

"Yes. At least forty of you, stacked one on top of the other. And in the fifty years since they built this particular challenge, how many folks have they lost?"

"None." She stood a touch taller, the tension lines in her face easing into a soft smile.

"Exactly. Now, on the count of three."

She took a visible breath and bent her knees once again, only this time in preparation to lunge.

She needed to do this. To finish strong, otherwise the very thing that was supposed to increase her confidence—and her trust in him—would only intensify her fear and create a sense of failure.

"One." The kids beneath them joined in. "Two. Three."

She raised her chin, eyes locked on his, and leaped straight into his arms.

"Yeah!" He closed his eyes as the cinnamon scent of her hair flooded his brain. Heart thudding so loudly he feared she might hear it, he looked into her beautiful brown eyes. He was reluctant to let her go but knew he needed to. He had no business holding her in the first place.

Cheers erupted from below, punctuated by a deep-voiced, "Woot-woot! Dominated!"

Blushing, she cleared her throat and gingerly stepped to the side, equally reluctant, it seemed, to release him.

As if she felt safe in his grasp. Safe with him.

In that moment when he'd held her, and she'd raised trusting eyes to his, his heart had told him there wasn't much he wouldn't do to keep her looking at him that way.

That was precisely why common sense urged him to keep his distance.

Chapter Eight

The next morning, Daria got the children settled with their toys and then opened her schedule book to the previous day. It appeared they'd had steady rentals from open to close. Plus, Jason hadn't called her once, which meant he either hadn't experienced any problems or had felt confident in addressing them. That meant she could leave him in charge more often, if need be. Until he left for college. But she'd deal with that when the time came.

She skimmed the notes she'd taken the day before. An image of Tyler standing on the final challenge platform, eyes locked on hers, hand extended, flashed through her mind. Her face heated at the memory of his strong, protective embrace. Her cheek pressed against his muscular chest. The steady beating of his heart beneath her ear and the way he'd looked at her—as if she had captured his attention completely.

Stop this. Thinking this way would only lead to heartache, and her heart had been pummeled enough.

Focus. She released a loud breath and rubbed her temples.

She needed to email Elias to thank him for sharing his time and, hopefully, get something scheduled for the weeks ahead. Although he'd seemed genuinely enthusiastic about the prospect of sending campers her way, she feared he'd deem her operation too small to accommodate his needs.

How much would her business improve if she hosted motocross competitions?

She turned to her computer and searched the internet for relevant sites. Interesting. There was a dirt bike and riding school for children in Conroe. If she went that route, she'd need to hire an instructor, but that'd generate income while she built a proper course.

She was halfway through an article on track design when her phone rang. She glanced at the screen and answered. "Ann. How are you?"

"Not as good as your littles are gonna be when you tell them my news."

"Cookie had her puppies?"

Nolan sprang out of his seat and to her side. Of course, Isla followed, and soon both children were tugging on her.

Ann chuckled. "Yes, ma'am. All eight of them."

"Wow. That's a lot."

"More than we need around here, that's for sure. If you're not busy, you and the kiddos can come over. Get some time with the critters."

"I've got a party of four scheduled to come in soon. After that, I'm free until late afternoon."

"Perfect. That gives me plenty of time to make a batch of marshmallow-cereal squares."

"You don't need to do that."

"All part of my campaign to become the children's favorite person. Although my son is quickly becoming a fierce competitor."

Tyler. The man who just yesterday had anchored her

with his steady, kind gaze and had encircled her trembling frame into his strong embrace. She could still hear the rhythmic thudding of his heart; could still feel the rise and fall of his rib cage as he breathed.

Had he said anything about their camp visit? About how fearful she had been, and how she'd practically thrown herself into his arms? He probably didn't consider that moment worth mentioning.

Nor should she.

She cleared her throat. "Nolan adores you both." The way he looked up at her with pleading eyes about guaranteed his complete lack of patience for the rest of the morning.

As expected, after the call, Nolan asked if they could go right then and there at least a dozen times, causing Daria to arrive at the farm frazzled and with two hyper children.

Ann was waiting for them on the porch. Smiling and waving, she hurried down the steps and greeted them each with a hug.

Daria glanced around for Tyler and then chastised herself for it.

How could she remain Ann's friend, come over here as often as she did, and watch him invest in the children, without falling for the man?

"Where is she, Nana Ann?" Nolan dashed in the direction of the stables, turned toward the chicken coop and then back around, looking like a child dropped in a toy store with an unlimited gift card.

Laughing, Ann took Isla's hand in hers. "This way, sweet cheeks."

Nolan walked beside her, ran ahead, and then came back around before skipping off again. By the time they reached the hay barn, he was out of breath and both children's faces were flushed.

As they were about to enter, Nolan blocked their way and gave Isla a stern look. "Shh." He held a finger to his mouth. "You have ta be quiet."

She imitated him, and then the two tiptoed toward the sound of yipping. Their stuttering steps accelerated as they grew closer until they rounded the corner. Seeing the mama dog lying on her side surrounded by her pups, Nolan seemed to lose all thought of approaching quietly and raced ahead. He slid to his knees about two feet away.

Isla toddled forward and then froze, eyes wide. "Babies?" Opening and closing her extended hands, she glanced back at Daria.

"That's right." She smiled and squatted to be eye level with the child. "Itty bitty, aren't they?"

"Mama?" She reached toward Cookie.

"Mmm-hmm."

Nolan turned hopeful eyes to Ann. "Can we hold them?"

Ann nodded. "But let me help you." She picked up a white one with patches of black, brought him to Nolan, and then sat beside him. "Lay your hands flat, palms up, in your lap."

"Like this?"

"Yep." She placed the puppy into his hands. Nolan sat stock-still, shoulders stiff, gaze locked on the wiggling, squeaking ball of fluff.

Cookie glanced their way and then rested her head back on the straw-covered floor as her babies squirmed and rooted their way to milk.

"Me, too?" Mimicking her brother's position but with opening and closing hands, Isla began to fuss. "Me, too?"

"Absolutely, sweetie." Daria brought her the largest of

the litter, keeping the creature in her hands, which she rested in her niece's lap. "Gentle."

Nolan scrunched down to kiss the puppy's head. "Can we keep him? Please?"

Daria rubbed his back. "Remember, we talked about this." She wasn't surprised this question had resurfaced. It was one thing to accept an answer regarding an idea of something. To do so while holding the adorable creature in one's lap was another matter entirely. Even she was struggling to maintain her firm no.

"I'll take good care of him and feed him and play with him and keep him in my room. Please? I love him so much."

"I won't debate this with you." Once they had their own place and a plot of land, she'd get the children a dog and some chickens. Maybe a bunny, too.

"Ahh." He slumped with a frown.

His sad eyes tugged on Daria's heart. While she suspected Lucy would concede if asked, bringing in a pet while they themselves were guests didn't feel right. "I know that's disappointing. You'd do a great job taking care of him." How could she explain that their home wasn't technically their home without creating insecurity? "But I said no."

Ann snapped her fingers. "I've got an idea. What if your auntie lets you keep this little guy at the farm? That way he can run and play in the pastures and sleep here in the hay, and you can tend to him when you come over."

Nolan's thin brows pinched together. "He'd still be mine?"

"All yours."

"I'd be his daddy?"

"Pretty much." She looked at Daria. "What do you say?"

She loved her friend's creative thinking and desire to bless the children. "Brilliant."

"Yay!" Nolan raised a fisted hand, his torso giving a little bounce. With a glance at the puppy now cockeyed in his lap, his expression sobered, and his body stilled. "Can I name him?"

Ann nodded. "'Course, sunshine. What're you thinking?"

He pinched his bottom lip between his thumb and index finger. "Squeaky?"

Daria laughed. "He does do a lot of that."

Nolan frowned. "When he gets bigger, he'll bark like Cookie?"

She exchanged an amused smile with Ann. "Probably."

Her nephew resumed his lip-pinching. "Chocolate? 'Cept he's white, too. Oreo?" He looked at Daria as if awaiting approval.

She smoothed his bangs from his face, the delight in his eyes filling her with joy. "Perfect."

He beamed and then hunched forward, his face close to his newfound friend. "Do you like that name, Oreo? Huh? Do you?" His tone carried the singsongy cadence with which he spoke to his sister.

Soon, Isla grew restless and occupied herself with a game of reaching toward the puppies as if to pet them, squealing, then toddling two to three feet away before repeating the motion.

Ann chuckled. "Doesn't take much to entertain that cutie-pie, does it?"

Daria smiled. "Out here, no, it does not." The children's doctor had encouraged her to expose them to as many sensory activities as possible, stating that it helped their mental and physical development. She could only imagine all the neurons firing in their brains whenever they spent time on the farm or experienced Ann's affection. "I really appreciate how you invest in my kiddos."

Ann's eyes danced. "I love them."

"And they love you." That was her greatest concern. She wanted the children to know without a doubt that they were valuable and loved. She understood the profound ache of not feeling those things. Thankfully, she'd found a great counselor in high school who'd helped her process those soul-deep wounds left from her broken childhood. Unfortunately, her sister had resisted therapy and chose self-destruction instead.

After years of self-destructive living, her sister was just beginning to turn her life around and had even begun to dream.

A lump lodged in Daria's throat. She cleared it away and focused on the wiggly bundles of fur snuggling close to Cookie's belly.

"Well…" Ann pushed to her feet with a grunt. "Best get to it. I need to bring the menfolk lunch. They started harvesting today, which means they won't be coming in from the fields till well after dusk."

"Tyler mentioned something yesterday on the drive home. I could tell he was anxious to get started." She rested a hand on Nolan's back. "Let's let Oreo spend time with his mama so he can eat."

Groaning, Nolan slumped. "Can we come back after?"

Daria tucked his tag into his shirt back. "I'm sorry, bud, but I need to return to work." Thankfully for her bank account, she had steady bookings from late afternoon until closing.

He crossed his arms, face puckered in an exaggerated frown.

"But I bet you can sit in the tractor with Mr. Tyler for a spell," Ann said. "When we bring him lunch."

Nolan's eyes brightened. "Really?"

Daria picked up Isla and brushed bits of hay from her clothes. "I would hate to get in his way."

"Nonsense." Ann waved a hand. "He'll welcome the short distraction, and he'll be plumb tickled to see this munchkin." Taking Nolan's hand, she led the way out of the barn and into the bright afternoon sun.

Daria fell into step beside her as they passed the goat pen.

"Little Nellie there looks like she's about ready to pop." Ann motioned toward a pregnant doe lying in the shade of the lean-to and then eyed a metal bucket over the top of the fence. "Looks like they could use more water." She jiggled Nolan's arm. "Want to help?"

"Yeah!" He gave a half skip, half jump, and followed her to a spigot and pail a few feet away.

Task completed, the four of them headed back toward the house, Ann pausing along the way to do this or that, always inviting one of the children to join. As a result, they didn't reach the kitchen until well after one.

She poured them each a chilled glass of lemonade. The children, cheeks red from their adventures in the heat, gulped theirs down. Sippy cup clutched in the crook of her arm, Isla sat on the ground with a plop and rubbed her eye with a fisted hand.

"Someone's tuckered out." Ann placed two plates, each with half a peanut butter and jelly sandwich and tomato slices, on the table, one in front of the high chair for Isla, the other for Nolan.

"She'll probably conk out the moment I get her settled into her car seat." Daria attempted to put her in the high chair, but Isla fought her. The child only grew more agitated until her fussing turned into an all-out tantrum.

Daria released a breath. Now what? She worried if

she tried to force her niece into the contraption, she'd accidentally hurt her.

"How about a picnic?" Wiping her hands on her napkin, Ann left. She returned with a blue blanket that she spread across the floor.

Isla clearly preferred this option. Crying softened into stuttered sniffles, and she began eating the sandwich in her fisted hand.

Daria wiped the child's nose with a tissue. "We may have to take a rain check on the tractor."

"No!" Nolan said. "You pwomised!"

That was his new favorite phrase, used regardless if warranted. Feeling her shoulders tighten, Daria took a slow breath and then turned to face him. "No, sweetie. I said…" That he could go, which was basically the same thing. She glanced at Isla with her droopy eyes and nodding head. "You can go another time."

"But you pwomised. You pwomised. You pwomised."

She feared he was about to throw a tantrum that would set off his sister once again. Then she'd have two wailing children, and with an emerging headache besides.

"I know what we'll do." Ann pulled a party-sized bag of potato chips from the pantry and tossed them into a massive carry-tote already filled with other food items. "How about you and Nolan take lunch to the menfolk while I stay with Isla. She can nap right here on the kitchen floor, or you can get her settled on the living room couch."

The idea was tempting. Much too tempting, considering how often her thoughts drifted to Tyler. An image flashed through her mind of him sitting tall and strong in the cab of a combine, his muscular shoulders and back straining against his T-shirt, kind laughter dancing in his eyes.

The very reason she did *not* need to be heading out to the fields.

She shook her head. "I'm sure you have better ways to spend your time than to sit around with a sleeping toddler."

"I've got plenty I can do right here while she naps." She indicated the kitchen with a sweep of her arm. "I didn't plan on finishing my outside chores until the temperature cools down a bit, anyway."

Before Daria could decline, Nolan leaped to his feet and started jumping while chanting, "Yay! Yay! Yay!"

Poor little Isla was so tired, she appeared completely oblivious to her brother's loud cheers.

"All right." Daria turned toward Ann. "If you're sure you don't mind."

"Not one iota. Just give me a minute to finish up with these." She motioned toward the slices of bread topped with mayonnaise and folded slices of turkey spread across the counter.

Daria washed her hands at the sink. "How can I help?"

"There's sliced cheese in the fridge."

Nodding, she immersed herself in sandwich making, hoping to awaken her more rational side. The part of her that remembered precisely how unavailable her friend's handsome, hardworking, and kind son was.

Tyler had barely reached the end of his row when an incoming call rang through his Bluetooth earbuds. Idling, he pulled his phone from the side door pocket and glanced at the return number. Uncle Jed. Maybe he was reaching out to offer a hand. He and Tyler's dad used to help one another. For a long time, they'd even shared equipment, which was a common way farmers worked together to reduce equipment costs.

Tyler had worried that arrangement had stopped once his dad left.

He answered. "Hello. Everything right as rain over in your neck?" He almost chuckled at the irony of his statement, considering this season's near-flooding downpour had very much *not* made things right for most Sage Creek farmers.

"You missing a donkey and a broodmare?"

"I don't…" He scrubbed a hand over his face. "You have a couple of animals wandering about?"

"Yep."

"How far'd they make it?"

"Onto the gravel road between your land and mine heading toward the highway. Might've reached it, too, if I hadn't been driving into town just now."

"Mind corralling them back onto my side of the fence?"

"Nope, although you might want to get over here when you get a chance. Someone left a bunch of beer bottles and fast-food wrappers lying around. Found your gate wide open, too, and more thick, wide treads, like last time."

In other words, more ATV riders. Tyler closed his eyes and pinched the bridge of his nose. "Okay. Thanks for letting me know."

"Did you ever talk to that gal who took over at Omar's place?"

"Yeah. Honestly, it could've been just about anyone. You know how many problems we farmers have had with teenagers over the years."

"Haven't seen anything other than her lime-green vehicles around here. Nor has anyone else."

"You asked around?"

"A bit."

"Okay, thanks." He appreciated how Uncle Jed was

trying to look out for his mom. "And thanks for getting my animals back where they belong."

"Might want to have another sit-down with the gal running the place."

Daria had assured him the problem wouldn't happen again. Could she really control how her renters behaved?

A door clanked shut on Uncle Jed's end. "This kind of garbage never occurred back when Omar held the reins."

If that was true, that meant Daria probably was to blame. Either she wasn't laying down the law clearly enough or folks didn't respect her enough to comply. The issue could be with that high school kid she had working for her, too. Took a level of maturity to hold your peers accountable—let alone to resist joining them in their she-nanigans. Daria probably couldn't afford to pay enough to hire an adult.

He kneaded a kink in his shoulder, reluctant to make her life any more difficult than it already was but wanting to do what was best for his mom. "I appreciate you keeping an eye on the place."

"With your dad gone, your brother off doing whatever it is he does, and you serving our country, I figured she could use someone watching out for her."

Although Tyler knew Uncle Jed didn't mean anything by it, the statement regarding his time in the Navy left a heavy feeling in his gut.

Uncle Jed made a hacking sound likely caused from a lifetime of heavy smoking. "Speaking of. Did your mama tell you what she and I talked about a month or so ago?"

"Regarding?"

"That farm's too big for her to run alone. I know you and your brother are here now, but I remember you not being too keen on working the land. Has that changed?"

"No." He didn't resent the place as much as he once

did, but harvesting crops had never been how he'd envisioned spending his adult years.

"I told your mama she might want to consider selling the place and getting herself a nice little condo somewhere."

"You and I are on the same page." Normally, he wouldn't speak so openly about his mom's business, but this wasn't some nosy neighbor looking for the latest gossip. This was Uncle Jed, a man his dad had often said he loved like a brother.

"All right, then. I best get to it." He ended the call.

With a sigh, Tyler looped the combine around. He was halfway down the next batch when a swirl of dust on the gravel road bisecting two fields caught his attention. His mom had promised to bring lunch this afternoon, only that wasn't her vehicle. It looked more like Daria's.

Why would she come out here? Did Uncle Jed call her? No. That wasn't his way. Even if he had, Tyler doubted she'd come out here to talk things out. And yet here she was.

He wasn't eager to engage in another conversation regarding irresponsible renters, and not just because he'd nearly made her cry the last time. He worried there might not be much she could do differently.

He was falling for her, and that was a problem, especially if it impacted his ability to hold an honest conversation that was in his mom's best interest.

He disengaged the combine, removed the ignition key, and climbed down. As he was crossing the field, Nolan raced toward him, his gait clumsy on the uneven ground.

The boy reached Tyler out of breath. "Nana Ann said I can ride in the tractor with you. Can I?"

He glanced toward Daria, who was unloading something, looked like his mom's tote, from her car's trunk. "What's your auntie say?"

"She said if it's okay with you. Can I?"

"Let's go have a chat with her." Tyler took the child's hand in his, and they walked the rest of the way together. Reaching Daria, he greeted her with a tip of his hat. "Hey."

"Hi." Her beautiful smile set him off-kilter, making him want to forget what Uncle Jed had told him moments ago. Not that he planned to broach that subject now, but neither could he avoid doing so indefinitely.

The breeze swept her soft floral scent toward him.

He took half a step back to keep his emotions in check and eyed his mom's blue-and-white polka-dotted tote that Daria had set on the ground. "You must've been put on lunch duty."

She laughed. "Something like that. On account of this munchkin." She ruffled Nolan's hair. "Your mom's staying back at the house with Isla while she naps."

"I imagine that didn't bother her none. Matter of fact, bet she insisted on it."

"Just about." She peeked into the tote. "Your mom made a lot of food. All this for you?"

He shook his head. "Probably wants me to share."

Her eyebrows shot up. "With us?"

"That and the harvesters." He motioned toward the fields.

Her cheeks bloomed pink. "Right. Of course."

Man, was she beautiful when embarrassed. Or delighted, or deep in thought, or simply breathing.

Thinking this way would only get him in trouble—and potentially challenge his mom's ability to sell the farm if it kept him from discussing the open gate and empty beer cans. It didn't surprise him that riders would act irresponsibly if they'd been drinking.

What if the animals had caused an accident? Someone could've been seriously hurt, and the horse or donkey could've been killed.

"You okay?"

He glanced up to find her studying him with a furrowed brow. "Just thinking." He unwrapped his sandwich and took a bite. "Y'all hungry?"

Nolan shook his head. "I'm not."

He chuckled. "Won't be until after the tractor ride, I take it."

Daria tucked a lock of wind-stirred hair behind her ears. "Your mom fed the kids before we left."

"And you?"

Gazing toward the other combines, she rubbed two fingers across her collarbone.

"My mom made more than enough, trust me. Especially if she knew you hadn't eaten before you left the house."

She accepted the sandwich he held out. "Thanks."

He nodded. "Did you get any rentals while we were at the camp yesterday?"

She grinned. "Business stayed steady about from open to close." Her smile evaporated. "If I didn't know better, I'd say, based on your expression, that you don't think that's a good thing. Am I reading you correctly?"

Gazing past her, he scratched his jaw. He hated to bring bad news. Resuming eye contact, he relayed his conversation with Uncle Jed.

"What makes you think my customers were to blame?" Her tone held a hint of a bite.

"It's just strange, is all, for all of this to be happening

now." He repeated Uncle Jed's comment regarding how things had been when Omar had run things.

"How would you know? You weren't here."

He flinched. Was that an accusation? A dig regarding his failure to help his mom? "A buddy told me."

She opened her mouth as if to give a retort and then took a visible breath. "I understand your concern. For your mom and the animals. I'll talk to Jason."

"Appreciate it."

And if her renters weren't to blame? If some rebellious teenager thought he could take advantage of a single mom business owner and newly divorced farm owner, assuming he could do whatever he wanted and they'd never know? That scenario seemed just as likely. Maybe more so.

Was Tyler simply looking for a way to exonerate her? He had to admit, he'd felt an urge to defend her while listening to Jed's accusations. Still, it wouldn't be right to blame her, or her riders, for something without proof.

But how could he get that? It wasn't like he could watch the gravel road or his mom's fence line 24-7.

He could put up a trail and hunting camera. He'd placed his in storage but had been wanting to buy a new one, anyway. This seemed the perfect excuse.

Tyler tossed his balled-up tinfoil into the tote and turned to Nolan. "Ready for that ride, little man?"

"Yeah!" Nolan bounced on the balls of his feet.

"Let's get after it, then."

The child reached up for his hand, but Tyler picked him up and draped him over his shoulder like a big old bag of grain. He could feel Daria's eyes on him as he carried the boy across the field.

He shouldn't have made that comment about Omar. If he were her, he probably would've felt attacked. Then again, if she was upset, could be that was for the best. Maybe if she showed him a cold shoulder, he'd be better able to keep his wits about him. Otherwise, it seemed like his heart and head would keep duking this out, and he'd lose no matter what he did.

Chapter Nine

Although business remained steady Wednesday morning, Daria managed to snag thirty minutes to take the children on "an adventure," as Nolan called it. Determined to catch a lizard, he brought his butterfly net and binoculars.

Daria loved his enthusiastic smile, which he seemed to be displaying more often now. Maybe the children getting cut from day care hadn't been such a bad thing, not in the interim, anyway. Although trying to keep them entertained created added stress at times, they also brought her a great deal of laughter.

Venturing onto a lesser-used mountain bike trail, they continued over exposed roots and potholes and around boulders. They stopped periodically so he could pick up a treasure or search beneath rotting logs for lizards.

They'd just turned back when her phone rang. She glanced at the number and answered. "Ann, hello."

"Hey, sugar. Want to drop Nolan off for a spell this afternoon so he can help me with the junk barn? Figured he might get a kick out of selling stuff at the antiques fair. He can have his own table right next to mine, of course."

"I imagine he would love that." Daria could envision

him standing as tall as his three feet and a quarter-inch frame would allow. Yet, while she did want Nolan to follow through on his part of his and Tyler's arrangement, she knew her nephew would take more of her friend's time than he would be helpful. "I love how intentional you are about spending time with the children, but I know you're super busy with your wheat fields and all."

"The boys have that covered. It's been nice seeing them work toward a common goal as a team for once. Plus, Tyler hired a local harvesting crew to help. They're knocking things out lickety-split."

"I remember." Wouldn't that cut into their profits? Not that it was any of her business, except she got the impression Ann wasn't doing so well financially.

"That a yes?"

She mentally reviewed her remaining rentals for the day. "I won't be able to come by until after seven." Would that be too close to their bedtime? Although her work schedule had begun to disrupt that, which was an area Daria wanted to improve. She'd heard children thrived on routine. She just needed to figure out how to establish that for Isla and Nolan, despite her often unpredictable and variable hours.

"That'll work."

Call ended, Daria slipped her phone into her back pocket and switched Isla, who felt heavier by the moment, to her other hip.

Would Tyler be around when she and the kids went to see Ann? Her pulse stuttered at the thought.

For someone trying so hard not to get swept off her feet, she sure spent a lot of time at his place.

She'd do well to remember his displeased expression when he'd told her about the unlatched gate, and the fact that he could easily limit her access to his mom's land.

As much as she wanted to believe Ann would never let that happen, Daria wasn't so sure. Not certain enough to bank her business on. Tyler was Ann's eldest, after all. His word carried a great deal of weight.

Was that really what concerned Daria? Or was she simply finding reasons to suppress her hope for more?

With a huff, she followed Nolan out of the woods, across the parking lot, and back into the office where she immersed herself in work while the children played.

Anything to distract her thoughts from Tyler.

By the end of her workday, she'd interviewed four prospective sitters and had held a more thorough conversation with the young lady who'd watched the children when she and Tyler visited the church camp. She'd also filled five notebook pages, front and back, with research related to opening an archery range.

Passing Ann's wheat fields half an hour later, she eyed the combines, three in total, making their way down the rows. They'd covered a lot of ground since lunch the day before.

"Look, Isla," Nolan said.

Daria glanced at her nephew through the rearview mirror.

He leaned forward in his seat, pointing. "I drove that."

Isla's eyes widened. "Me, too?"

He shook his head. "You've got to be a big kid. Like me."

Daria pulled her lips in over her teeth to keep from laughing and turned onto the Reyeses' property.

Nolan tugged on the back of Daria's seat. "Can we see Oreo?"

"Briefly. But then we need to get to work."

"Then horse riding."

"Probably not today, buddy. Besides, you haven't earned back your first lesson."

Crossing his arms, he released a sigh that must've completely emptied his lungs. Once again hiding her amusement, she parked and shot Ann a text to let her know they'd meet her in the junk barn shortly.

Unfortunately, her concession did nothing to appease her nephew. After a few minutes with the puppies, he became so reluctant to leave, she worried he'd throw a fit. But then a field mouse darting out from some hay bales captured his attention. He sprang to his feet and raced after it. Not fast enough. By the time they stepped into the early evening sun, the creature had disappeared, likely into the nearby pasture.

"Let's go find Nana Ann." Carrying Isla, she took Nolan's hand and led him to the dilapidated building housing at least a century's worth of items.

Ann had formed a pile of toys, camping gear, and other smallish objects just inside the door. She greeted them each with a hug and then propped her hands on her hips. "Thought I should pull the safe stuff out so the little guy doesn't accidentally happen upon a rusted nail or sharp edge." Her cheeks were red, and beads of sweat glimmered on her nose and forehead.

"I appreciate that."

"There are some things buried in the loft—an old wagon and a tricycle—I think the children would enjoy. I asked Tyler to come carry stuff down."

He was much too busy for that. "I appreciate the thought, but—"

"Hush, now. He's coming to help, and that's all there is to it. Pretty sure he's getting ready to quit for the day, anyway."

Daria doubted he'd want to spend what little time off

he had digging through a bunch of antiques, but she'd be rude to argue the matter.

Ann opened one of her large totes and pulled out a plastic container of marshmallow-cereal squares. "You kiddos hungry?"

Nolan nodded, and he and Isla both hurried over.

"Figured so." She retrieved a tub of disposable wipes from her bag and handed them to Daria. "Didn't think you wanted sticky hands gathering all this dirt and grime."

Daria smiled. "You're always so prepared." And well-kept, whether working in the kitchen, mucking stables, or poking around a dusty old barn.

"Do I get one of those?"

Daria startled at the familiar deep voice. She turned to see Tyler leaning a shoulder against the door frame. His clothes bore a day's worth of wheat dust, and his face held a tinge of sun that epitomized the phrase *rugged good looks*.

"One, yes." Ann shot him a pointed look. "Three tops." She handed him a treat.

He bit off half, and with a playful grin, made like he wanted to snatch the whole container.

She smacked his hand and made eye contact with Daria. "I've got to watch this one. He could polish off this entire batch if I let him."

Based on his broad shoulders, chiseled biceps, and sleek stomach, every bite went straight to muscle.

She sensed him watching her assess his physique and, face hot, quickly looked away.

"Hey, little man." He held out his hand for a fist bump. When Nolan simply stared at it, clearly confused, Tyler switched to a high five. Popping the remainder of his marshmallow square into his mouth, Tyler turned to Isla. "Hello, Princess." He grabbed her by the torso, swung her giggling body into the air, and then set her back to her feet. Thumb hooked in his belt buckle, he looked around. "What'd you need me to do?"

Ann set a checked photo box onto a wicker seat with torn spikes. "Up there." She pointed to the loft crammed with stuff from nearly top to bottom. "Your father placed a lot of my old playthings in that far back corner. Some were passed down from my grandmother, and her mother before her." She listed off numerous items. "I thought Nolan might want to give my old wagon a good scrubbing and sell it. Or keep it for himself, if he'd rather."

His eyes lit. "To pull Oreo?"

Ann laughed. "Sweetie, you can use it however you want."

"Speaking of buried treasures…" Tyler strode down the barn aisle, stepped behind a stack of wooden wagon wheels resting against a support beam, and returned with a child-sized cowboy hat. He smacked it against his thigh, releasing a swirl of dust that tickled Daria's nose. He punched out a dent in the crown and placed it on Nolan's head. "Every horseman needs a hat and a wagon."

Hand to the brim, her nephew stretched an inch taller. "Can I give the puppies a ride tonight?"

Daria placed a hand on his shoulder. "Remember why you're here."

The child slumped with a forceful sigh.

Mouth twitching as if fighting a smile, Tyler left to retrieve the requested items. A handful of trips later, he'd brought down everything Ann had requested along with two large plastic tubs and a basket of chubby children's books.

Once Nolan became engaged with washing the wagon, Tyler leaned toward Daria, hand cupped over his mouth.

"I can swing him by the stables right quick before y'all leave tonight."

"You don't have to do that. I know you must be exhausted."

"I've got to check on our foals, anyway. Then tomorrow, I can give little man a short lesson."

"I really appreciate your willingness to spend time with him, but there's no rush. I realize this is your busy season."

"We've got a lot of folks helping. Besides, I want to get him off to a good start, at least enough for him to figure out if he'd like to learn more, before I leave."

Before I leave.

The words formed a knot in her gut.

With an internal sigh, she quickly shifted her thoughts to Nolan. He'd had such fun last time Tyler had worked with him. He'd chattered the entire drive home, barely stopping to catch his breath. She'd noticed a stark change in his mood as well. She could tell he still missed his mama, and probably always would. Yet, he didn't seem nearly so angry all the time.

Every boy needed a positive male role model, and he clearly adored Tyler. She feared too much.

How would Nolan respond once the man said his goodbyes?

Something Lucy said to her years prior when she'd been struggling to let people in came to mind. *Trying to protect yourself from getting hurt doesn't work, sweet girl. All that does is bar you from joy, leaving you with a dull ache in your soul that could last a lifetime.*

She'd promised herself she wouldn't teach the children the same self-sabotaging lessons the foster care system had taught her and her sister. She would encourage them to embrace all the blessings life had to offer for however long each lasted.

She'd once promised herself that she'd do the same.

But that was before she met Tyler Reyes, the man who could easily shatter her heart if she let him.

Tyler had only been in the barn for about twenty minutes when his mom announced that it was time for supper.

Wesley's car was gone by the time they all made it back to the house. Apparently, he was meeting a woman he'd been dating. Tyler had overheard one of the guys they'd hired to help with the harvest ribbing him about it. Interesting that Wesley hadn't brought the gal to the house for dinner. Made Tyler wonder what kind of woman she was and if she was as irresponsible as his brother.

At least Wesley had put in an honest day's work in the fields. With help from him, some guys from church, and the harvesting crew Tyler had hired, he expected they'd be done by late tomorrow afternoon.

While Daria helped his mom in the kitchen, he took Nolan to see the foals. In the summer, the horses received all the nutrition they needed from grazing, so he didn't need to feed them. As to the other animals, he shot Wesley a text asking if he'd tend to them so he wouldn't have to rush through his stable visit with Nolan or supper afterward.

He told himself he merely wanted to be polite. It wasn't that he wanted to spend more time with the children and their beautiful aunt. But with every encounter, his logical justifications for his behavior when it came to those three felt unconvincing.

He was falling for the woman, despite his efforts to the contrary.

Nolan talked nonstop the entire way to the stables,

wanting to know what dinosaur was fastest, meanest, or strongest, or might make the better pet.

"Can't say that's something I've thought much about," Tyler said.

"The Stwuthiomimus can run sixty miles an hour."

"Never heard of that one." He wasn't sure he'd recognize the name even without Nolan's lisp.

"They had a beak like an ostrich and walked on two legs like us. And they had short arms and a long tail. So that they didn't fall over."

"Sort of like a T. rex?"

"But not as mean, uncuz they only ate bugs and stuff."

"I see. What about the T. rex? How fast did he run?"

Tiny lines etched across Nolan's forehead. "Slower than a car, that's all I know."

Tyler chuckled. "That slow, huh?"

"Would you like one for a pet?"

"Wouldn't he try to eat me?"

"Not if you were his daddy, silly."

"I s'pose not."

Maribel, their oldest broodmare, galloped toward them as they approached the pasture. Three others followed close behind. Felt odd not to have Cookie underfoot, although they'd likely be dodging her puppies soon enough.

Ginger hung back, grazing beneath the shade of a tall Texas ash. Two other foals frolicked and played with one another in the center of the pasture. Then the smaller of the two reared up, tail high, and pranced to his mother.

Maribel nibbled on Tyler's shoulder.

"Hey, there, girl." He scratched her withers, causing her to wiggle and twitch her lips. "You looking for something sweet?" He turned to Nolan. "Think we should give Ms. Maribel here a peppermint?"

Nolan's eyes widened. "She likes candy?"

"Loves it. What do you say?"

He nodded, his wide grin bunching his cheeks.

Taking Nolan's hand, Tyler led the way into the barn and to the tack room where his mom kept grain, saddles, blankets, and whatnot. Looked like this place hadn't been tidied in some time. An old coffee canister holding peppermints sat on a top shelf.

He dug out a handful and gave half to Nolan. "Figured we should get some for the others, too. Don't want them to get jealous."

Nolan stared at the red-and-white striped candies and licked his lips.

Sure was a cute little guy. "You want one?"

Again, Nolan nodded. He fought with the outer wrapper, dropping the others onto the ground.

"Let me help." Tyler tore open the plastic and then handed it back. He motioned toward the door. "After you, cowboy."

Nolan touched his hat and puffed out his chest. Walking with a Clint Eastwood swagger, the boy led the way out. Soon, all the horses and foals gathered along the fence, anxious for a treat.

"Hello, little mama." Tyler ran his hand down LuLu's muzzle. "Glad to see you've taken to your youngin'. Had me worried for a bit."

"Which one is her baby?"

He pointed. "That little guy with the band of white."

"Does he have a daddy?"

"He does. But we keep him in a different pasture."

"Whycome?"

"He can be a bit of a bully."

Nolan frowned. "Ms. Kendra says I'm a bully. Do you think I am?" He looked up with hopeful, sad eyes.

"No, little man. You're just a kid who's had to deal with a lot of hard things."

"Like my mama dying?"

A lump lodged in his chest. "Yeah, like that." He wished he had the words to comfort the poor kid. He'd once read an article that said simply being present was enough. Maybe it was more that there was nothing else a person could really do. No words to make such a loss stop hurting. Sometimes wisdom came in knowing when not to speak.

And so he didn't. He just stood with his arm gently draped around Nolan's small shoulders, letting the boy process whatever emotions these dams and foals had stirred up.

An owl hooted from somewhere within the distant woods, and the steady chirp of crickets and birds created a harmony of sound he'd always found soothing. As a teen, he'd spent many an evening right here in this spot, trying to reconcile the peace he experienced with the horses with the increasing pressure he felt to help run the farm. Seemed that had been the expectation from as far back as he could remember. For a long time, he'd felt like he hadn't a say in the matter or other options.

Until the day the Navy recruiter came to his school. The military had seemed like the answer to all his problems. He soon came to realize, however, that he'd merely exchanged one set of challenges for another. Not that he viewed his time in the service as a waste. Every drill, battle, and tour of duty had built within him the confidence and grit to overcome whatever difficulties life threw his way.

That included getting his mom out from under this place without losing her last dime.

One of the foals wedged his way to the front and nibbled Nolan's shoulder. The boy jerked back with a squeal that ended in a giggle.

"Guess he thought you looked tastier, huh, little man?" He tousled Nolan's hair, glad to see a spark of joy return to his eyes.

"Is it their suppertime?"

"Nope. But I bet it's ours. You ready to head back?"

He frowned, and for a moment, Tyler thought he'd say no. But then he slipped his tiny hand in Tyler's, and they strolled together down the gravel road the way they'd come. The setting sun haloed the house in golden light, reflecting off wispy clouds in streaks of red, purple, and orange. A faint crescent moon hung above the hilly horizon.

They returned to find Daria and his mom sitting at the picnic table beneath her old oak. Isla sat in the grass nearby, placing colorful foam shapes onto a multi-pegged board.

Tyler surveyed the assortment of food, place settings, and glasses of iced lemonade. "What's this?"

"It's such a beautiful night, thought we'd eat outside for a change," his mom said.

His gaze shot to Daria. Her soft smile and the way the setting sun cast a gentle glow upon her delicate features captivated him.

She turned to Nolan. "Did you have fun?"

He nodded and relayed everything they'd done in detail, barely pausing between sentences to catch a breath.

She raised her eyebrows. "Wow. You did all that?" She and Tyler exchanged an amused smile, and the gratitude in her eyes made him feel two inches taller.

Had he ever encountered a woman so beautiful? And not just in how she looked. It was her gentle nature, the way she smiled with her entire presence, the soft cadence of her voice, and the tender way she engaged with her nephew.

He cleared his throat and looked away. "Sure smells good." He sat across from his mom, kitty-corner to Daria so that she wouldn't be in his direct line of sight. Hopefully, that would help him rein in his emotions before they took hold of him.

"I was telling Daria about the time your brother decided he wanted to enter the Settler Day's hot-dog-eating contest. You convinced him to pay you, in advance, to coach him, on account your stomach was so much bigger than his and all."

Chuckling, he grabbed a corn-bread muffin from the basket in the center of the table. "Most relaxing two days of my childhood." He made eye contact with Daria. "We didn't have an allowance back then, so he agreed to do all my chores for a week. That must've seemed like a steal to him, considering the winner earned something like fifty dollars."

His mom nodded. "A lot of money for any seven-year-old, but even more so back then when a person could buy a candy bar for thirty-five cents."

"You should've seen your face when you came home to find him on his hands and knees on the porch eating out of the dog bowl. While the dog just sat there, watching, probably wondering when he'd get a turn."

"Or if there'd be any left." Shaking her head, she turned to Daria. "Tyler had brought the entire bag out, ready to refill."

Tyler laughed so hard that tears sprang to his eyes. "He'd already had one whole bowl full."

Daria gasped. "Do you mean you trained your brother using dog food?"

Tyler gave a slight shrug, hands out, palms raised.

His mom made a mock frown. "Wasn't he simply terrible?"

"I was just a smart entrepreneur."

"Your father didn't see it that way, and not for your lack of trying." She buttered a muffin. "Tyler tried to convince him that he was helping us save money on groceries."

Daria turned her dancing eyes to him, captivating him with her unrestrained smile and the pink flush to her cheeks. She made it all but impossible for him to look away.

Not that he wanted to.

Matter of fact, he'd be quite content to spend the rest of the evening, and a thousand besides, right here at this table with her.

That was a dangerous reality he needed to fight, before his rebellious heart caused him to lose all common sense.

Chapter Ten

Pleasantly full, Daria leaned back in her chair, amused by Ann and Tyler's playful banter. These were the types of meals she'd always longed for as a kid. The deep connection shared between a parent and their son or daughter. This place provided a sense of familial peace and belonging she'd believed, for a long time, didn't exist outside of television.

Then she'd met Lucy. Although Daria had never found the father she'd always ached for, Lucy had more than filled the hole left by her biological mother. It felt like something of a full-circle moment to think that she was now trying to do the same for Isla and Nolan. And she had the support of Lucy and Ann, two surrogate grandmothers, for the children to rely on.

If only Tyler wasn't set on leaving...

Then what? They'd fall in love and enjoy a lifetime of happily-ever-after? She wasn't sure that would ever exist for her. She hadn't exactly had a plethora of role models in that department. Lucy had been the only healthy adult in Daria's life growing up, and she'd been single.

Isla started fussing and pushing against her high chair's tray. "Down pwease! Down pwease!"

Daria laughed. "All right, sweet girl." She picked Isla up and sat her on the lawn in front of the toys Ann had brought out for both children.

As the sun dipped below the horizon, framing the distant hills in a faint glow, stars emerged in the inky sky. Fireflies flashed and buzzed about, disappearing into the grass and then reemerging. Nolan chased after them, first this way and then that. Daria retrieved his butterfly net from the car, and Ann brought out an empty mason jar. This occupied Nolan and entertained the rest of them for a good fifteen minutes before he flopped onto the ground, breathless.

Isla began rubbing her eyes.

"Looks like the kiddos have about reached their limit." Daria approached her niece with open arms, picked her up, and squeezed her close. "You ready for story time, munchkin?"

"Story time?" Ann stood. "I haven't enjoyed a good ol' snuggly, cuddly story time in some twenty years." She caressed the child's cheek, making eye contact with Daria. "Would you mind? I've got some picture books I used to read to Tyler and Wesley tucked away in a box inside."

"I appreciate the offer—"

"It's not an offer, sugar. It's a request." She darted off before Daria could say anything further.

Tyler stood and began clearing the table. "You probably know by now, once she gets an idea in her head, there's no uprooting it. Especially when it comes to these cuties, it seems." He loaded himself down with a stack of dirty dishes.

"She's been amazing."

"I 'spect she'd say the same about you all."

Daria followed him inside, reflecting on the first day she'd met Ann. Having recently taken over Off Roadin'

It, she'd been trying to connect with all the neighboring property owners, hoping those who'd allowed Omar to pay for the use of their land would let her do the same. Having moved from a Chicago suburb, she was used to people wanting to keep conversations with strangers short and to the point.

She hadn't realized how cordial the people of Sage Creek were. Nearly everyone, including those who'd denied her request, had invited her in for sweet tea and a baked good of some sort.

When Ann learned about Isla and Nolan, she'd asked Daria back the next day, insisting she bring the children. Then the day after that. Initially, Daria had accepted for fear of appearing impolite and damaging a potential business connection. She'd soon realized how lonely the woman was. Not long after, what had begun as an act of compassion blossomed into a genuine friendship.

"You okay?" Tyler's voice broke through her thoughts.

She smiled. "Perfect."

They'd soon cleared the table and Ann was settled on the couch with a child under each arm, book spread between them.

Passing back through the living room, Tyler paused. "Princess's eyelids sure look mighty heavy. I'll be surprised if she makes it through a full book."

The sight warmed Daria. "I agree. Thankfully, both children can sleep through just about anything, including getting loaded into the car and then back out and into bed."

His mom glanced up with a stern expression contradicted by the mirth in her eyes. "Y'all go enjoy this beautiful night and leave us be."

Tyler raised his hands, palms out. "Yes, ma'am."

He shot Daria a wink that sent a rush of heat through

her. Walking faster to hide her blush, she pushed through the screen door to the porch, where she lingered, gazing toward the stars glimmering in the sky.

Tyler stepped beside her, close enough that she could feel his warmth and his familiar leathery citrus scent. He was close enough that she worried he could hear her heart thudding in her chest.

"Sure is peaceful here."

"It is." He sat on the top step. "I used to come out here a lot when I was a kid. Usually when my father and I couldn't see eye to eye on something."

She joined him on the step, one leg bent, chin resting on her knee. "Did you and he get along when you were growing up?"

"Not really. I mean, I wanted to, just not enough to do what he wanted, I guess." He gave a half laugh, half snort.

"You don't strike me as the rebellious type."

"More like headstrong. He and I disagreed on who should get to decide what I did for the rest of my life. He felt I should stick around and help him and Mom on the farm, and I wanted to live anywhere else."

"Sounds like you really disliked it here."

"I'm not sure if it was that as much as I hated him thinking he had the right to decide for me." He released a breath. "I can now see he and Mom just needed help. From the looks of things, my dad didn't want to farm any more than I did. This place wouldn't be in such a mess otherwise."

"It's that bad?" Was she being nosy to ask? Except she got the sense that perhaps he wanted to talk. Or maybe she was just hoping that was the case—that she wasn't the only one wanting to connect on a deeper level. What she really needed was to be focusing on doing the opposite.

There was no sense pretending she was merely being

a friend. She feared her heart would never settle for that, not with Tyler Reyes.

"Our fields are yielding more than I anticipated, so that's good. But the current price per bushel hasn't been this low since 2010."

"I've heard people say the market's been tough on farmers for a while now."

"That's true, especially with more and more crops being produced by big corporations. I guess I shouldn't be too upset with my dad for leaving. The farm. Not my mom. I'm plenty mad about that. Although I have a feeling he tried talking her into going with him."

"Into selling, you mean?"

"Yeah. But she probably dug her heels in. She feels like she has to keep the farm going. Did she tell you how she got it?"

"From her great-aunts?"

He nodded. "Their parents, who owned the land before them, didn't have any sons, so when they died, they left everything to their daughters. The ladies never married or had children of their own."

"They ran the farm by themselves?"

"They did their fair share, but no. They hired folks. Gave them room, board, and a decent salary. Or so I'm told."

"Did the workers stay at the house?"

"The men? No. Back then, that would've been quite the scandal, no matter how those ladies explained it. They used to have a one-room building filled with bunks or whatnot. 'Course, most of those fellas were seasonal and used to sleeping wherever they could."

"Fascinating." She loved hearing about how people once lived and what they chose to pass down. "Sounds like this place has quite the history."

"On winter evenings, when things slowed down crops-wise, my mom used to take me and my brother to the barn of disarray as she calls it. A lot of that stuff came from my dad's antique hunting. But my mom kept a fair number of family heirlooms, over half from the aunts. Some from their mama or papa before them."

She fiddled with her bracelet, the only true family keepsake she owned. "My bio mom gave me this the day I graduated high school."

"You and she stayed in contact?"

"I tried for a while. She wasn't that interested in quote unquote jumping through the ridiculous hoops the state required. In the beginning, she visited about once a month. Then twice a year. Once child protective services terminated her parental rights, she quit coming around and sent postcards instead."

"I'm sorry. That must've really hurt." In the glow of the porch light, his eyes radiated a depth of compassion that made her want to share more.

"It was hard." She blinked back tears. "Especially the day I got this." She lifted her arm to indicate the jewelry. "Mainly because she said she'd come. I knew better than to believe her. She'd made and broken so many promises. But I'd always told myself that was the state's fault. That she truly loved me and wanted to see me but my caseworker made it too hard."

He inched closer so that his hip touched hers and placed his strong arm around her shoulder.

She tensed, and for a moment, she felt a pull to shut down, to push him away, suppress her feelings, and change the conversation to something more pleasant. A topic that showed her strength, not the day that had nearly broken her. But she also craved the support Tyler offered, knowing he wasn't asking for anything in return. He was just here, listening. As if he truly cared.

"But?" His voice was low, husky.

She leaned deeper into his embrace, soothed by the steady beating of his heart. A heart that felt, in this moment, completely focused on her. She couldn't remember a time when she'd felt that from a man. Or felt safe enough to share her deepest hurts.

"I'd already finished my classes the fall prior." Her chest felt heavy. "I was working a full-time job and had a studio apartment by then."

"So you were basically on your own."

She nodded. "Which means my mom didn't have to break through any bureaucratic red tape or get past anyone trying to keeping her from me."

"And she didn't show."

"She mailed me this bracelet with a note telling me how proud she was of me, how much she loved me, and how she wished with everything within her—" Her voice cracked. "Those were her actual words. That she wished with everything within her that she could come to my graduation. Instead, she bought me jewelry." She closed her hand around her bracelet. "And wrote a letter stating how expensive it was and how hard she'd worked to earn the money to buy it."

"I'm so very sorry." He tucked her hair behind her ear, his knuckles grazing the side of her face.

"You want to know what's really pathetic?"

He didn't respond.

"I kept it." A sob wretched from her throat. "I've worn this every day since. I don't know why. I don't even like jewelry much. But this is all I have of the mother who didn't love me enough to show up. That's all I wanted. For her to just show up. Was that too much to ask?" Tears slid down her cheeks. Her mom had disappeared from her life completely not long after.

"Shh." He cupped her chin in his hands and turned her head so that her eyes met his. "That's not pathetic." Moisture glimmered in his eyes as he thumbed away her tears. "You needed your mom."

"Lucy helped fill that void." As had Ann. The faithful love and support she regularly received from both helped soothe her deepest wound. "But it still hurts."

"I suspect that's an ache that never goes away, no matter how much a person tries to talk themselves out of it."

She was beginning to think the same about Tyler. That her longing to stay near him, to build something precious with him, wouldn't lessen, regardless of how hard she fought it.

Worse, she wasn't sure she wanted to keep resisting, even though she knew she'd be completely devastated once he left.

And if he chose to remain in Sage Creek? Was there any chance of that? If his greatest issue had been with his dad, maybe he could change his mind. He loved his mom, and he clearly wanted to see the farm thrive. Otherwise, he wouldn't be working so hard to fix it up or finish the harvest.

Would he stay, not just for his mom, but for her as well?

They sat in silence, her leaning against his chest, tucked within his comforting embrace. His breath was slow and steady, matching hers. If she ever fell in love, she was certain the relationship would involve moments just like this. Where she and the man she loved could gaze at the night sky, watching stars disappear behind the clouds and then reemerge. Neither feeling compelled to fill the silence.

She could've easily remained where she was, held by Tyler indefinitely, if not for the children. Inhaling, she slid out from under Tyler's arm and stood. "I best free your mom from the kiddos."

He rose, his eyes studying hers as if he wanted her to stay as much as she did. Then he nodded, stepped back, and opened the door for her.

Inside, they found the children and Ann asleep on the couch. Isla and Nolan were turned toward their surrogate grandmother, each with a cheek on her chest. Ann's head rested on top of Nolan's, her arms around both children, a storybook in her lap.

Emotions still raw from the previous conversation, the sight pricked and soothed the gaping hole her mother had left. Growing up, how many times had she longed for what God had given the children in Ann and Lucy? Through them, and hopefully through Daria as well, He was breaking chains of generational dysfunction. By His grace, Isla and Nolan would never feel the cavernous hole of aloneness she and her sister had.

"I've got the little man." Tenderness filled Tyler's voice. He walked forward, slid his arms under Nolan, and gently lifted him up. With the child's head flopped against his shoulder, he followed Daria out to her car. She opened the back passenger door and the booster arm for him. Nolan's eyes fluttered open and then he closed them again, muttering something about a brontosaurus.

Tyler chuckled. "That little guy's brain never stops, does it?"

His affectionate tone was like balm to her heart. She shook her head and led the way back inside for Isla.

With both children buckled in, Tyler rounded her car to the driver's side and opened the door for her. "Come back tomorrow for Nolan's next riding lesson?"

She gave a slight smile, feeling vulnerable and exposed but also safe. "If you're sure you've got time, he'd love that." As would she.

"It's a date." Grinning, he gave a quick, strong nod and then shut her door.

A date. His words hung in her mind like an aptly spoken promise, although she knew he didn't mean them that way. But maybe one day he would.

She returned to Lucy's to find the house dark except for the porch light and a soft glow emanating from the kitchen. Daria tucked the children into their beds and seeing them with their blankets under their chins filled her with a sense of gratitude so profound her chest burned.

In her room, she knelt beside her bed and rested her forehead on folded hands. "Father, You have given me so much. Blessings I've always wanted but that felt so out of reach for so long." She thought about the verse from Psalm 139 that said all her days were recorded in God's book before one of them came to be.

Tears of gratitude and praise pricked her eyes. "You saw this moment all along. When I felt abandoned, unloved and unlovable, and as if nothing would ever change, You truly were working all things out for my good. For Nolan's and Isla's good as well. Thank You for holding on to me, for placing me in Lucy's home so long ago, and for bringing me to Sage Creek."

The next morning, she drove to work well-rested and filled with a sense of hope she hadn't felt in some time, if ever.

Parking beneath the shade of some trees, she glanced at the children chattering in the back seat and smiled. Today was going to be a great day, regardless of how many customers came in.

Halfway across the lot, her phone rang. Purse draped

over one shoulder, a large tote of toys over the other, and both hands filled, she hurried into her office and dropped her things on the floor.

Drake's name flashed on her screen.

Answering, she nudged Isla inside. "Good morning." Did she sound too eager? She took in a slow, deep breath and donned her most professional tone. "How can I help you?"

"I'm calling to see if you've got room for a bunch of my kids, and potentially a handful of adult leaders, to-morrow. We were supposed to go tubing down the river, but apparently, we never confirmed or something, and another group took our slot. Now I've got a gaggle of students that will be sorely disappointed if I don't find an alternative."

And he thought they'd consider driving around on ATVs a good trade? Lucy would tell her not to under-value herself. To stand tall and confident in the gifts and opportunities God provided. Regardless, she needed this business—as much of it as she could accommodate, any-way. Would the fact that she didn't have enough vehicles for the whole group dissuade Drake?

Then again, he already knew how much equipment she owned. She chewed her bottom lip and turned the page on her appointment book. "You probably remember, but I've only got four ATVs and three UTVs."

"ATVs are for single riders, right?"

"Correct. The UTVs can sit up to four."

"And dirt bikes?"

"I've got five."

"Perfect. We'll give those to our most energetic stu-dents." He laughed. "Wear them out so they can't get into any mischief."

She thought of Drake's warning regarding the youth's

potential rowdiness and need for supervision. After the two problems her renters had already caused him and Ann, she wanted to be extra careful. She certainly didn't need her customers causing any more issues.

She poised a pencil over her appointment book. "How many adults?"

"Counting my wife and I, we should have three."

"What time?"

"Maybe 11:30?"

"I've got you down. See you tomorrow." Smiling, she ended the call, picked Isla up, and danced around her office with her niece on her hip. "Things are looking up, baby girl." Best part was, if the teens had fun, they'd be back. They might even bring their friends with them.

Nolan sprang to his feet and hurried toward her.

"Want to join us?" She clutched one of his hands and spun him in a circle. Nolan giggled, Isla happily squealed, and Daria laughed. Moments like these made all the hard work, uncertainty, and frustration worth it.

She started to text Tyler and then stopped. Since when had he become the first person she contacted when receiving good news? Except it only made sense to share this with him, right? He was, after all, the one who'd connected her with Drake.

She clicked on his contact and stared at the cursor flashing on her screen. After a few typed and then deleted messages, she finally sent a quick, Thanks for the youth group lead. Drake just called to reserve a slot.

His response came almost immediately: Awesome!

The sense of affirmation his text provided triggered a smile.

Her next goal was getting on that church camp's must-do list.

The rest of her day was steady enough to stave off

boredom but not so busy that she wasn't able to tend to the children. With the promise of more business ahead, she closed that evening more encouraged than she'd felt in some time. She could do this. She could run a successful business and raise happy and well-adjusted kids. *Thank You, Jesus!*

Her phone rang as she was strapping Isla into her car seat. Tyler's name flashed on the screen, and a wave of warmth swept through her. She smiled and answered through her Bluetooth. "Tyler. Hello."

"Hi. I'm heading to the stables to work with our foals and wondered what time you thought y'all might get here."

"I'm actually heading there now. If that's okay?"

"Yep. You hungry?"

Turning onto the highway, she glanced at the time on her car's dash. Seven thirty. Ann had probably already served and cleaned up after supper. "We had a late lunch, followed by a plethora of snacks."

Apparently, the prospect of increased bookings gave her the munchies, because she'd eaten more today than she had in the previous two combined. It was more likely that her earlier worries about her business had suppressed her appetite.

"Home baked, I'm guessing?"

She laughed. "We may have enjoyed our fair share of your mom's zucchini bread. And apple spice muffins. And snickerdoodle cookies."

"Nolan should be all nice and calm, then?"

"Oh." Her smile evaporated. "No. I mean, yes, I'll make sure he behaves. If at any time he—"

"I'm joking. He can bring all his energy and then some."

She released a breath, her tense shoulders relaxing. "Thanks for that." No wonder Nolan adored Tyler.

She was beginning to feel the same. The scary thing

was that she no longer felt so compelled to fight her feelings. That meant she was either heading fast toward heartbreak or the type of relationship she'd always wanted but had assumed didn't exist, at least, not for her.

Chapter Eleven

Tyler heard Nolan before he saw him, and it sounded like his mom had joined him and Daria. With how much she loved those children, he knew she'd come watch one of Nolan's lessons eventually.

She'd miss the kids when she left with him, and they'd miss her. The thought made him question if he was doing the right thing pushing her to move to Omaha. But she couldn't stay here, unless maybe she sold the farm and found another way to support herself. It wouldn't be easy entering the job market, Sage Creek's especially, in her midfifties without much work history.

Nor could he adequately support them both if he stayed. Sure, he could turn a wrench, but they already had a town mechanic. He could hire on as someone's hand or planting manager, but he'd left that life behind the day he joined the military.

Even if he could revitalize this place so his mom actually started turning a profit, how long would that last? Until the next wheat disease, drought, or hailstorm destroyed their crops? Besides, he planned to get married one day. When that time came, he wanted more to offer a woman than a dying farm, debt, and an uncertain future.

No. He and his mom needed to move to Nebraska. He may not have done so great watching out for her before, but he intended to do better now. The transition might be hard at first, but they'd recover.

"Mr. Tyler! Mr. Tyler!" The steadily approaching footfalls suggested Nolan was running.

"Walk, please." Daria's tone was stern.

A moment later, the child emerged, and with a sharp turn, made to run into the stall.

Tyler blocked his way. "Hold on, little man." Hand on the boy's shoulder, he squatted down to eye level. "Remember what I told you about approaching a horse?"

Nolan's gaze shot to Ginger, who stood perpendicular to them eating hay. Brow furrowed, he looked back at Tyler and nodded. "Don't sneak up on her."

"That's right. You need to come at her from where she can see you, otherwise she'll get spooked."

His gaze dropped to the floor. "I forgot."

He ruffled the boy's hair. "I understand." He stood to greet Daria, Isla, and his mom.

"Guess this is the effect of all that sugar I fed him this afternoon, huh?" Daria laughed.

"Either that or it's a result of his enthusiasm to go riding." Tyler tickled Isla under her chin.

"Oh, there's that for sure." His mom bopped Nolan on the nose. "The child could hardly get here fast enough."

"Well, then, guess we best get started." Tyler grabbed a halter and lead rope from a hook outside the stall. "Let's review our safety rules."

He noted Daria's stiff posture. Poor woman was terrified of horses. He'd hoped watching how careful he'd been with Nolan last time would alleviate her concerns.

How would she respond once he left and handed over the reins, literally, to someone else?

After his normal, pre-riding spiel, he fastened a helmet onto Nolan's head. Then he tacked Ginger up, led her into the corral, and helped the child into the saddle.

Nolan tugged at the straps buckled beneath his chin. "This makes my head hot."

"I know, buddy, but you need to protect your noggin." He tapped the helmet with his knuckles.

"Uncuz I'm so smart?"

"Exactly." He and Daria exchanged an amused smile, making him feel like they'd shared a moment. He handed Nolan the reins. "Sit tall, shoulders down and relaxed." Poor kid looked as stiff as the railing he was climbing on a moment ago. "Elbows bent, thumbs up, wrists facing each other." He guided Nolan's hands and then his body into the proper position. "That's right. Perfect."

After a few more reminders, Tyler led him around the corral, instructing him as they went. The boy paid close attention and was a quick learner.

"Ginger is bored of going in circles." Nolan gazed off toward the distant trees beyond.

Tyler chuckled. "She is, is she?"

He nodded. "She wants to go faster. You have to go fast for goat tying, right, Mr. Tyler?"

"Correct."

"As fast as Stwuthiomimus?"

"Remind me again, how fast did they run?"

"Like a car."

"One driving down Main Street, a dirt road, or the highway heading to town?"

Nolan's thin brows pinched together, and he didn't respond right away. "Like a cheetah or a wildebeest."

Daria laughed, a melodious sound he'd never tire of. "Lucy brought home a new animal encyclopedia from the library, and it's become Nolan's latest obsession, other than dinosaurs, of course."

That boy was something else. "You've sure got a lot of facts stored in that brain of yours. Once you start school, you'll give your teachers a run for their money."

"Does Ginger like running?"

Tyler smiled. "She does. Horses need plenty of exercise to stay happy and healthy."

"She wants to run. Can we?"

Ah. That was what the boy was driving toward. Daria mentioned how much the child loved exploring. Tyler had been the same growing up. For all its frustrations, the farm had provided him with plenty of opportunities for exploring. He had fond memories of the wind in his face, sun on his back, and the steady thumping of a horse's hooves galloping through an open field.

"You'll get there." He glanced at Nolan's leg to make sure he was keeping his knee against the saddle. "Just give it time."

"Nana Lucy says I catch on quick. That means I learn fast. Only she hasn't seen me on horses. Do I learn fast on Ginger, Mr. Tyler?"

"You're a natural, little man."

Nolan raised his chin. "That's uncuz I'm a cowboy."

Tyler chuckled. "I can see that."

"'Cept I don't know much about cows. Cowboys have to know a lot about cows, right? Do you know a lot about cows, Mr. Tyler?"

"A bit."

"Have you ridden on one before?"

Tyler's eyebrows shot up, and his mouth twitched toward a smile. "Can't say that I have. Not sure they'd take too kindly to that."

His mom laughed. "That would be a sight. Although he did ride a goat once, didn't you, son?"

"Now there's a memory."

"That's my kind of riding." Daria's statement reminded him of her fear of horses. A fear he should probably help her conquer so she wouldn't pass it off to Nolan or Isla.

His mom must have been thinking something similar, because she said, "You know, Daria, it'd be a shame for you to spend all your time watching others do the riding. You should let Tyler give you some lessons."

"Oh, no." She raised her hands, palms out. "I would hate to encroach on Nolan's time with Tyler."

"Don't be silly." Ann took Isla from Daria's arms. "The kids and I need to go check on the puppies, anyway, don't we, kiddo?" She made eye contact with Nolan.

He frowned and shook his head. "But it's my turn. I want to go faster."

Tyler knew if he didn't intervene, the moment could be lost, and Daria might never take the opportunity to overcome a fear. "Remember, you're a cowboy, and a cowboy is always a gentleman."

"What does that mean?"

"That they give their auntie a turn with the horse." His mom leveled a firm gaze at the boy. "That's the kind thing to do, right?"

"But I'm not done." Tears welling in his eyes, his body tensed as if he were using every muscle to cling to the horse. "I want to go faster and learn to tie goats and ride on the road and in the woods. It's still my turn."

Daria looked from Tyler to Nolan and then back to him. "I appreciate—"

His mom quieted Daria with a hand on her shoulder. "Nolan Anthony Ellis, that's not how gentlemen behave.

You know good and well that you've had a turn. Twice now, in fact, while your auntie hasn't been on once."

"She doesn't want to, do you, Auntie?"

Daria took a visible breath, and her nervous expression turned stern. "Remember what we talked about this morning about minding your elders?"

Tyler suspected her response had less to do with her wanting to ride and was more about not wanting to reinforce negative behaviors. He respected that.

Nolan huffed. "I know, but—"

"Besides," his mom said, "I could use your help in the barn of disarray. The antiques fair will be here before we know it. You won't make much money if you don't clean up more items to sell. What's that you're wanting to buy?"

"A park for dinosaurs," he said, his tongue tripping over the *s* and *r.*

"That's right." She snapped her fingers. "With volcanoes, trees, and boulders. Can you imagine all the fun you'll have with that?"

The child's scowl softened.

"Wow." Tyler gently lifted Nolan off the horse and set him on his feet. "We never had anything that cool when I was a kid." Hand to the back of his head, he guided the child toward the fence.

"This is true." Ann watched Nolan climb through the bottom and second railing. "Although I bet I've got some pretty cool toys tucked away in that barn somewhere. Let's grab your auntie a helmet and go take a look."

Daria watched them disappear into the barn and then turned back to Tyler with a slight shake of her head. "Your mom is impressive."

"How so?"

"She not only stopped a tantrum before it started, but

she actually made Nolan excited to obey. I feel like I get a parenting class every time I come here."

"Guess my brother and I trained her right, huh?"

"As in exposed her to every stressful scenario possible?" There was that adorable dimple again.

"Exactly."

"Seriously, though. Your mom always knows what to say when. Whereas I'm continually second-guessing myself."

"Seems like you're doing a pretty good job to me."

"Thanks. I try. Although I didn't have the best role models growing up. At least, not until Lucy. Sometimes the pressure… It just feels like a lot, you know?"

"I hear you. Whenever one of my Navy buddies or I got hung up on what-ifs or regrets, our sergeant used to say, 'All you can do is make the best decision possible based on the information and resources you have.' Figure that's part of what it means to live in grace. Just do your best and trust the good Lord to make up for your lack."

His mom returned with an adult-sized helmet that she handed to Daria. Then, with a cheerful wave, she and the children headed back down the hard-packed dirt road toward the house.

Tyler scratched Ginger's withers. "Want to pet her?"

"Sure." Daria rubbed the horse's neck, and as she did, her stiff posture relaxed. "She's so beautiful."

"The definition of a gentle giant. Want to give her a peppermint?" He produced one from his pocket.

Humor lit her eyes. "Nolan said he fed her candy, but I thought he was just telling one of his stories."

"He likes to tell tales, does he?"

"A bit, but not because he's trying to be dishonest. I think he gets so caught up in his make-believe world, he forgets what's real and what isn't."

He continued to engage her in light conversation, watching as her tense expression eased into a soft smile. Once certain she felt comfortable, he said, "You ready?"

She pulled her hair back with both hands and released it, then nodded.

"Hold on here." He placed her hands on the horn of the saddle. "Put your left foot into the stirrup, push up, and swing your other leg over."

"Okay." She did as instructed, only requiring a gentle lift from him. Shoulders and arms stiff once again, she released a breath.

"That's it. Don't squeeze her." He tapped her knee and repeated the same basic posture instructions he'd reminded Nolan of moments before. "We'll circle the corral some. Then, if you're up for it, we can go for a ride across the property." He noticed her stiffen once again. "Only if you're ready."

"Okay."

He didn't want to push her, but he also knew her fear would grow if not confronted. Still, although he had a lot of equine experience, he hadn't spent much time teaching humans to ride, and none of them had displayed fear. Nor did he know why Daria was so afraid.

This seemed uncharacteristic of the type of woman who would embrace single parenting and move with her ready-made family to a new town to run an outdoor adventure business. Only thing he could figure was that she'd had a bad experience.

He thought back to their time at the Christian camp. She'd been nervous then, too, but she had overcome it. The look of victory on her face when he'd held her in his arms assured him she considered her prior discomfort worth it. Had he not encouraged her to keep going, she would've missed out on a powerful confidence builder.

If he didn't push her now, while he had the opportunity to walk beside her, she could remain afraid of horses for the rest of her life. Then, not only would she risk passing her fear on to Nolan, she could forfeit an amazing experience as well.

Everyone needed to feel the freedom of the wind on their face as they galloped across an open field.

He led Daria and Ginger back into the corral. "You ever been riding before?"

"Once."

"Your expression makes me think that it wasn't the best experience."

She huffed. "Hardly. I was about seven and living with an older couple that didn't seem to like kids much. For some reason, my sister was placed with someone else. Nowadays, the state tries to keep siblings together, but back then, things were different. I'd only been with this couple a month when they took me with them to a family reunion out in the country."

"In Illinois?"

"Probably. The property owners had a blind pig, a donkey, some free-range chickens, two big dogs, and a couple horses. And there were a lot of kids of all ages. I didn't know which ones belonged to who. They all seemed comfortable around the animals. I'd never been in that type of environment before and wasn't sure how to act. But I wanted to fit in, so I pretended like I knew what I was doing."

He cringed. "I think I know where this is headed."

"If you're picturing me shoeless and bareback on a horse, then you'd be right."

"And the adults?"

"No idea, but not with us. There were a few teenagers, but they were mostly trying to show off for one another, which didn't help."

"How'd you get on?"

"Honestly, I don't remember. Climbed up the fence or something? Anyway, by then I think the horse had about had enough. Either that or he could tell how clueless and terrified I was."

"They can—" He clamped his mouth shut. Telling her horses could sense a person's fear wouldn't increase her confidence. "They can sure seem quite large to a child."

"True. Anyway, he started going fast pretty much from the moment I got on. I was holding on for dear life, screaming for him to stop, to whoa. Whatever I could think of. That only made him madder."

She had probably been squeezing him with her legs, a signal to go forward. If so, her verbal commands to stop would've confused him. "He bucked you off?"

She nodded. "But that wasn't the worst part. What bothered me most was how the older kids reacted. They got angry at me, telling me I was being a baby and would get them in trouble if I didn't shut up. I know now they were probably scared about how the adults would react to them letting us younger kids ride unsupervised. All I knew was that I was hurt and in a strange place with strange people who didn't seem to care what happened to me." She sniffed and wiped a tear from her cheek.

"I'm sorry." Anger toward those kids welled up within him.

"Actually, I think this is good. Me riding tonight and remembering that even, I mean. I didn't put it all together until now. That was a season of my life I'd never fully processed. Maybe it's not horses I'm afraid of. Maybe it's more the sense of aloneness and vulnerability I felt that summer."

And she'd shared that deeply personal story with him. Did that mean she felt safe with him—that she trusted him with her pain?

With her heart?

The thought squeezed the breath from him.

And when he and his mom left? How would Daria respond then? She'd already endured so much. He hated to think that he would soon be the source of more pain.

What if he asked her to come to Omaha with them? Would she? With how much she seemed to love it in this small, rural community, would that even be fair to ask?

His smartest move would be to put some distance between them in the hope that it would decrease the emotional pull he felt toward her. Instead, he'd just invited her on an evening horseback ride across his mom's property.

Daria gazed across the field. The sun had begun to dip below the horizon, casting the distant hills in a fiery glow and painting the sky in streaks of orange, purple, and red. "It's going to be dark soon."

Tyler nodded. "But the full moon will give us plenty of light. If you've never seen a pasture bathed in its silvery gleam, you're in for a treat. I don't know if there's anything quite so gorgeous. Plus, horses have excellent night vision, and we'll stay on the property, so we won't have to worry about oncoming cars or anything."

Chewing her bottom lip, she tried to picture what the landscape might look like once night swallowed the remnants of the sun. If nature's canvas was anything like some of the paintings she'd seen over the years, the scenery would be magical.

And so very romantic. The type of experience she'd always remember, with the potential to capture her heart for good, and not only regarding the land.

If only Tyler planned to stay. Had he ever entertained the option, even for a moment?

She suppressed a sigh and refocused on her original concern—the apprehension Ginger stirred within her.

She looked at Tyler. "How far were you thinking of going?"

"Up to you. We can stop and head back whenever you want."

When would she have another chance like this? If she didn't take it, she'd probably regret it. With Tyler's departure rapidly approaching, tonight could be one of their last together.

She thought about a cliché a former social worker used to repeat with every new placement. *You know what they say. It's better to have loved and lost than to have never loved at all.*

While Daria wasn't fully convinced of that statement, she'd learned a sad truth from watching her sister and her adult relationships. Trying to protect herself from getting hurt, she'd closed her heart to joy as well. What's more, she'd merely exchanged the potential pain she feared she'd experience for the ache of self-induced isolation.

Daria would not follow in her sister's embittered footsteps.

Besides, she'd already grown too attached to Tyler Reyes to keep him from taking her heart with him when he left. With a painful goodbye all but guaranteed, she might as well fully enjoy every moonlit moment.

She made eye contact with Tyler once again. "Let's do it."

"Yeah!"

His broad grin made her think that perhaps he was beginning to care for her as much as she was starting to care for him.

Ten minutes later, they were riding side-by-side through pasture left fallow. A gentle breeze caressed her face and stirred the ankle-high grass. Behind them, a barn owl's high-pitched vibrato harmonized with the steady chirping of crickets and the thumping of the horses' hooves.

She cast him a sideways glance. "My time with you has been quite self-revealing."

"How so?"

"Prior to the camp challenge course and riding today, I would've considered myself a courageous person."

"Seems to me you've proven that true."

"What do you mean?"

"Courage isn't about not feeling afraid. It's about not letting your fears get the final say."

"I like that." Somehow Tyler brought out the best in her while inspiring her to become even better. He seemed to have the same effect on Nolan.

"It's so peaceful out here." She gazed toward the inky, cloudless sky dotted with the first emerging stars. She thought she could make out Jupiter hovering above the trees.

"I came out here often as a kid. To clear my head. And sometimes my folks would let my buddies and I build a bonfire over near the pond. I should bring you and the kids out for s'mores sometime."

Except he'd be leaving soon, and just when they were beginning to connect. Once again, she could feel her old defense mechanisms rising—the desire to create emotional distance and self-protect. She couldn't let her fears of future pain rob her of joy in the present.

Easier said than done.

"This was always one of my favorite spots." Tyler pointed to a large oak a few feet ahead. "I'd sit for hours watching as the sun played hide-and-seek with the clouds or sank behind the trees. You want to stop here for a spell?"

"Sure." Anything to extend their time together.

He dismounted and came to her side. Offering one hand for support, he placed the other firmly but gently on her waist and helped her down.

Her lungs filled with his musky scent as she slid to the ground, and into his arms. Her heart beat so quickly that her chest ached. His eyes latched onto hers and then dropped to her mouth, his breath warm on her face.

Did he want to kiss her?

But then he straightened, released her, and stepped back. She couldn't deny her disappointment.

Leaving their horses grazing a few feet away, he sat at the base of the tree and leaned against the trunk.

She took a moment to regain her bearings and then sat beside him. They remained like that for some time, neither speaking, gazing at the darkening sky now full of stars.

Tyler plucked a long blade of grass and snapped it in two. "How's little man doing? He seems less angry lately."

"I've noticed that, too. I think his time out here with you, your mom, the horses, and the puppies have really helped."

"It's got to be tough for him to grieve his mama without fully understanding why she's gone."

"Lucy wonders if he's also working through attachment wounds from some of the ways my sister parented. She loved the kids but was always trying to fill up the holes our nonexistent father left by chasing after some guy. She'd get so wrapped up in whoever she was with, or wanted to be with, that she'd forget about Nolan and Isla."

"I'm sorry."

Daria would make sure they always knew they were her top priority.

Yet, here she was, after dark and with a man, just like her sister. Except she'd left the children with someone who loved them. They'd probably had a wonderful evening filled with puppies, crayons, sugar, and stories. No doubt they'd be snuggled on the couch next to Ann, fast asleep, when she and Tyler returned.

Besides, unlike her sister's boyfriends, Tyler actually paid attention to the children.

Which is why they'd become so attached.

That also meant that she wouldn't be the only one heartbroken when Tyler left. What if his departure undid the healing Nolan had only begun to experience? Was she being selfish and irresponsible to come over as frequently as she did?

Chapter Twelve

The next morning, Daria arrived at Off Roadin' It later than anticipated and feeling frazzled. She'd expected the children to stay home with Lucy and so hadn't worried about getting them up, fed, and ready, or getting snacks or anything packed.

But then as she was about to leave, Lucy had received an emergency phone call. One of her friends was experiencing gut pain intense enough to warrant a doctor's visit and make her reluctant to drive. Daria assumed the woman was suffering from some sort of stomach bug, and that Lucy would pick up the children before lunch. Even so, the last-minute change of plans had left her scrambling to get the kids fed and out the door.

Today was supposed to be one of her busiest days of the season. Hopefully, if things went well with Trinity Faith's youth, Drake would rent with her again. Plus, if the students and chaperones had fun, they'd tell others about their experience. Everything Daria had read indicated the effectiveness of word-of-mouth advertising.

She'd just sent a newly married couple out on an ATV when Tyler's truck pulled into the lot, spiking her pulse.

Toning down her overly enthusiastic smile, she waited

for him to park and gather what looked like a measuring tool from his pickup bed.

He reached her wearing that easygoing grin she'd come to love. "Hey."

"Good morning."

He glanced at the blue sedan sitting under the shade of a large maple tree. "Good to see you've got customers already."

She nodded and explained who they were. "The husband called last week to ask if there was a good picnicking spot on the property. He wanted to surprise his wife, but she caught on pretty quickly when she saw his soft-pack cooler. He tried to play it off as drinks, but she wasn't buying it."

His lighthearted expression flashed a momentary frown.

She remembered their conversation regarding the opened gate and trash. "Don't worry. He knows alcohol isn't allowed." And he appeared to be the type to follow the rules.

Tyler gave a nod. "I finished morning chores early. Figured I'd use the spare time to make good on my promise to measure your land."

"I'm sure you have plenty of other tasks to attend to." Not that she was in a hurry to send him away.

"Nah. It'll give me a chance to get some steps in."

She laughed. "Right. As if you need extra exercise."

"Mr. Tyler!" Nolan came running toward them with a book in hand. As usual, Isla toddled after him.

"What do you have there, little man?" Tyler dropped to one knee and placed an arm around Nolan's shoulder.

"I got this from the library." On the cover was a cartoon of a child holding a lasso and wearing a hat three sizes too big. Beside him stood a confused bull with a red-and-black checked bandanna around his neck.

The skin around Tyler's eyes crinkled as he read the title. "*Cowboy Bootcamp*, huh?"

Nolan nodded and began turning pages. "Did you know the people who got paid to work on a ranch weren't cowboys?"

Tyler raised an eyebrow. "Really?"

"Yeah. Uncuz they were called cowpokes. Only now that's not a nice name uncuz it means to be lazy and stuff." He flipped to another page. "And when they had to ride a long way—called a cattle drive—they brought a cook. A boy, though. Not a girl. Probably since girls don't like to get dirty and stuff. Except for Auntie Daria. She likes to dig and run and go exploring, just like me."

It looked like Tyler was struggling to keep a straight face. "She sure sounds like cowboy material to me." Making eye contact with Daria, he stood. "It's supposed to rain this evening, so we probably don't want to do riding lessons tonight. I wondered if you'd like to go to dinner instead."

Nolan raised his big, bright eyes. "Can I get chicken nuggets? And French fries with ketchup to dip them in? And ice cream after? With sprinkles."

Tyler chuckled. "You think all that will fit in your belly, huh?"

Standing taller, Nolan nodded. "Nana Lucy says I like to eat."

"A cowboy's got to keep his energy up, for sure." He slipped a hand into his pocket. "But how about you hang out with Nana Ann this time? Bet she'll whip up a batch of sugar cookies for you and Isla to decorate."

Warmth swept through Daria's chest. Was Tyler asking her out? Just the two of them, like on a real date?

Nolan frowned. "I don't want to stay with Nana Ann. I want to come with you."

Tyler's gaze shot to Daria, as if awaiting her response. "We can all go another time." She kept her voice soft. "How does that sound?"

Nolan's frown deepened. "But I want to go tonight."

Daria leveled her gaze on her nephew. "That's enough."

"We can watch the weather and set our next riding lessons accordingly," Tyler said. "Do like we did last time. I'll take Nolan for a few loops around the corral and then the munchkins can entertain my mom while you and I hit the trails."

Nolan raised big, hopeful eyes. "I want to go."

"We'll hang out before," Tyler said. "Then Nana Ann will get to spend some time with you and Isla."

Scowling, he crossed his arms. "I don't want to."

Tyler ruffled his hair. "Taking turns is hard, isn't it?"

"Auntie was my friend first."

Daria frowned. "Nolan." Although it felt awkward to force him to share in this instance, she couldn't leave his selfish attitude unchecked. "Remember what we read in your Bible devotions last night? About how Jesus wants us to show love to others?"

He stomped his foot. "It's not fair."

"This isn't up for discussion." She kept her tone firm but kind. "Would you rather go back to the office to make a toothpick and marshmallow tower or play with your dinosaur set?"

"Neither."

"Let me rephrase. Would you prefer to find something to do in the office so I can get back to work and Mr. Tyler can finish what he came to do, or do you want to visit the time-out chair?"

Nolan stomped off with a groan.

Isla toddled toward the parking lot. Daria picked her up and faced Tyler. "Sorry about that."

He waved a hand. "He's a kid. I get it." He glanced toward the trees. "Guess I best get at it."

"I appreciate this."

"My pleasure."

If not for the youth group coming, she'd offer to join him. There was something romantic about walking along a wooded trail with the man she loved.

The thought jolted her, but she couldn't deny the truth. The way he'd been looking at her a moment ago, as if there was nowhere else he'd rather be, suggested maybe he felt the same.

There'd been a time when she'd been afraid to hope, especially in regard to relationships. Her former therapist would call this growth.

If Tyler's plans to move to Omaha didn't change, would she still call her willingness to open her heart, even if timidly, a sign of healing?

Now wasn't the time for introspection. She headed back to the office to tackle her growing to-do list while keeping the children occupied.

She'd barely pulled up her email inbox when Lucy called.

Handing Isla the sippy cup that had rolled across the floor, Daria answered. "Hey. Everything okay?"

"Unfortunately, no. They're sending Gina to the hospital in Houston, and I agreed to drive her."

"Oh, no." That meant she'd probably be gone all day. Daria winced. How selfish could she be? This was obviously a crisis for Lucy's friend, and her first thought had been about how the situation would affect her?

"I'm sorry. I know this is a busy day for you," Lucy said.

"Please, don't worry about me. The kids and I will

be fine. Really." Things might become more hectic than
she'd like, but there were obviously worse things a person could deal with. "Is there anything I can do to help?"

"Just pray? She might have a colon obstruction."

"Absolutely."

Unfortunately, the rest of Daria's morning only wors-
ened. First, her internet quit working. That meant she
couldn't process credit cards and had to take down payment information manually. She feared that made her
seem unprofessional. Then Nolan bumped into her arm,
causing her to spill lukewarm coffee on her blouse.
Thankfully, she found an old T-shirt in the trunk of her
car. Not so thankfully, it had more wrinkles than an el-
derly pug.

By the time Drake and his crew arrived half an hour
later, she'd developed an intense headache and Isla
had grown fussy. If she put Isla in her playpen as she'd
planned, her whimpers would turn into a full-on wail.
"Come here, baby girl."

Picking Isla up, she turned to greet the energetic youth
and began collecting permission slips while she waited
for the adults to trickle in. "Welcome. How many more
are we expecting?"

Drake handed her a credit card. "We're good to go."
He pulled his phone from his back pocket, grabbed a slip
of paper with the name of the GPS app she used, and
started tapping his screen. "I thought some of our other
leaders were going to join us, but they couldn't make it."

She rotated to address the group. "All riders sixteen
and under must remain with an adult."

"Nope." A tall kid near the door shook his head. "I've
been riding since I was a freshman."

The girl standing beside him rolled her eyes. "That's
because you live on a farm, doofus."

"He's right," another student chimed in. "By law, only those under the age of fourteen need babysitters."

Apparently, the students found this hilarious, because his comment led to giggling, teasing, and a few play punches.

"I can supervise." A teen with spiked blond hair and a mischievous grin raised his hand. "I'm eighteen."

"With the maturity of a ten-year-old." The kid standing next to the blond slapped the bill of his friend's ball cap.

The kid made an I-see-you gesture. "Mud-bombing, dude. You're going down."

What did that mean?

"Uh-uh." Drake narrowed his gaze on the kid. "There will be none of that, or any other shenanigans, today."

The group moaned, and someone muttered, "No fun."

Their goofy banter made Daria a bit nervous. But while she didn't know Drake and his wife well, she trusted they had the situation handled.

Drake stuck his fingers in his mouth and whistled. "Y'all pipe down and pay attention to the lady."

When the students complied, he motioned for Daria to speak.

"Thank you." She distributed the rent-one-get-one coupons she'd created and then explained her rules and regulations. Based on the questions the kids asked, however, less than half of them actually listened.

As they all milled outside, she fell into step beside Drake. "They've got a lot of energy, huh?"

"They're a tad excited. Along with some teenage pea-cocking."

"Some what?"

"Boys and girls showing off for one another." Faith, Drake's wife, shook her head.

"Oh." Hopefully, that wouldn't push them to act stupid.

She was overthinking things because of her conversation with Tyler the other day. For all she knew, someone else was to blame for the litter and opened gate. It made a whole lot more sense that some local hoodlums were out causing trouble.

Regardless of who had caused the issues, his accusation still stung.

Tyler recorded his distance calculations into his phone's note app and turned back toward Daria's office. She had plenty of space to work with and could set up an archery range with minimal effort. She could also host birthday parties and whatnot. That would be easier than trying to set up a motocross course, something most folks wouldn't take kindly to.

He thought again about the recent incidents on his mom's property and who might be to blame. Jed had mentioned seeing a green jeep in the vicinity. That wasn't proof that one of Daria's renters was responsible for the incidents on his mom's land. And it wasn't right to make accusations based on hunches, which was why he'd placed his hunting camera up prior to coming here.

Either the vandalism would stop, or he'd know who the culprit was soon enough.

The temperature dropped a good ten degrees as he stepped into the shade of the trees. A bird, it sounded like a scissor-tailed flycatcher, sang from within the thickly clustered trees. An unseen animal stirred the vine-snarled shrubs to his right and a branch dipped and then sprang back into place.

He soon reached a T in the path. On his left it led to a clearing of knee-high grass interspersed with fragrant sumac, and to his right was a wooden plank spanning a dry stream. He continued past a rotting trunk decorated with a bouquet of yellow-cream mushrooms.

Laughing voices flowed toward him moments before three teenaged boys came zipping around the corner on mountain bikes. He darted out of the way as the kids, wide-eyed, veered around him and into the bushes.

"Dude!" The teen at the rear untangled himself from his bike, which he propped between his legs to brush dirt, pebbles, and dried leaves from his hands. "Sorry about that."

"Hey, that's on me." Tyler glanced in the direction from which they'd come, wondering how many others might soon barrel through. "I should've known not to go walking down a path meant for bikes." He grinned. "How many more of you are there?"

The tallest of the three, a youth with long blond bangs spilling from his helmet and into his face, shrugged. "Not sure who went where."

Tyler nodded. "Have fun." He was glad to see teens enjoying some good, clean fun. And staying on a designated path. Hopefully, the others in their group were as well.

He turned toward the wider and less encumbered dirt road meant for ATVs. Unfortunately, with only periodic patches of shade, this meant trekking the rest of the way in direct sunshine. As a result, he arrived back at the parking lot hot and thirsty enough to drink an entire gallon of sweet tea.

Maybe he could talk Daria and the kids into joining him for a quick root beer float in town. Was that too much, having just asked her out to Wilma's? But he *was* thirsty.

If their date went well, maybe he'd have the courage to broach the subject of their future.

A handful of students, four guys and two girls, were

engaged in what looked like a modified game of ultimate Frisbee.

He stopped a few feet away. "Y'all weren't interested in riding?"

A short kid shrugged. "Got here too late."

"I see." He was glad to know Daria had experienced an increase in business through the youth group. That had to ease Daria's mind some. Although that could make it hard for her to get away.

He popped his head into her office to issue an invite, anyway.

She glanced at the clock on the wall, then to Isla, who was playing with stackable ice cream shapes. "Lucy was going to take the kids to the Literary Sweet Spot for crafts and story time but had an emergency. I promised to take them instead."

Nolan's head popped up. "Can I get a treat? A cake pop or hot chocolate or a big cookie with candy in it?"

Daria smiled. "Yes, you may."

"I'll join you." Had he just invited himself to a preschool event? *Way to reveal your eagerness, bro.* But the words were out, and he only slightly regretted them. Although that could change if she shot him down.

Daria studied him. "You sure you want to spend the afternoon in a room full of children, most of whom don't have much experience sitting still? And who will probably be displaying the effects of eating some type of sugary treat?"

"Sounds entertaining."

"Oh, I'm sure it will be."

Man, how he loved her soft laugh. "What time?"

"Two thirty."

"Perfect." That would allow him to meet the farrier

when he showed up on his mom's farm. With a tip of his hat, he turned and strolled back to his truck.

He also promised his mom he'd look at her pickup to see why it kept making a grinding, clanking sound. If he were to guess, her transmission was going out. Depending on whether he bought used or new, that could run anywhere from a few hundred dollars to over a thousand.

Regardless, she'd need her own vehicle once they moved to Omaha.

And if she—and he—stayed here in Sage Creek with the woman he loved?

Despite how hard he'd fought against it, he did love Daria. He'd never felt this way about a woman before.

He wondered once again about asking her to move with him and his mom to Omaha. It had rural areas as well, along with numerous parks and bike trails for her and the children to enjoy. She could always run an ATV business there. She might even have an easier time renting to city folks, many of whom may never have gone off-roading before. He doubted she'd been in Sage Creek long enough to put down roots or form deep connections, other than with Lucy and his mom. And she'd still have his mom.

And him.

Would she consider leaving for him? Was it even fair of him to ask?

With a sigh, he accelerated onto the two-lane highway leading back to the farm.

Later, he strolled into the Literary Sweet Spot twenty minutes early. He grabbed a copy of the newspaper from an empty table and found an unoccupied armchair near the magazines to wait for Daria and the kids.

He flipped to the sports section to read up on his favorite baseball team. They'd finally broken their five-game losing streak, thanks in part to their new coach.

"Tyler, hello."

He turned to see Gabrielle, the Realtor he'd been talking to, striding toward him. She had short, brown hair styled to one side and wore white slacks and a puffy green blouse.

He stood to greet her. "Hi." They shook hands.

"You mind?" She motioned to an adjacent chair angled toward his.

"Please."

"How are things going at your mom's?"

He scratched his jaw. "With the harvest and all, I haven't made as much progress fixing things up as I'd hoped."

"Understandable. Like I mentioned when we last spoke, there's not really a best time to list a farm. Although most sell sometime between October and April."

"After harvest but before planting season. Makes sense."

"But I also remember that you were hoping to put it on the market by month's end. I was able to pull some comparables. I don't have them with me now, obviously, but as I stated previously, I expect you'll have no problem finding a qualified buyer. Of course, the more you're able to spruce things up, the better, especially if you decide to split up the land and sell the house to someone looking to homestead."

She glanced toward a display of various greeting cards. "I should probably take care of what I came in here to do—find items for a housewarming basket I'm making for some clients. Newlyweds. Just purchased their first house. Isn't that sweet?" She smiled. "It was great seeing you." They shook hands again. "I'll shoot you an email within the next few days to schedule a walk-through of your place. That way, I can help you focus on repairing those things that'll get you the most bang for your buck, as they say."

She turned and left before he could reply or fully process his thoughts and emotions.

So much had changed since he'd first spoken with Gabrielle. He was no longer certain he wanted his mom to sell. In fact, he was fairly confident that he didn't. He was also sure he didn't want to take that job in Omaha, not when he could stay here with the woman he loved.

What about his house? If he backed out now, he'd lose his deposit.

A guy could always earn more money, but he'd never meet another woman like Daria. Of that, he was certain. He had a feeling that if he walked away, he'd regret it for the rest of his life.

Hopefully, his friend who had pulled so many strings to get him the opportunity would understand. He'd call him tomorrow.

What if He brought you back to Sage Creek to help me save the farm? The statement his mom had made when he first returned replayed through his mind.

If she was right, if God had brought him here to stay, then nothing else mattered. Nothing but following His lead. That and holding on tightly to the woman he loved and the children he adored.

He'd long prayed for a family of his own, but he'd always assumed that would happen much later. Once he was settled in Omaha and at his new job.

Could it be that God was answering his prayer through Daria and the children?

His phone rang. His shoulders tensed when he saw the

name of the caller. Uncle Jed. Lately, he'd only called for one reason. He released a breath and answered. "Hello."

"Afternoon. I hate to be the bearer of bad news yet again, but I was driving home from the hardware store and saw your mama's gate, same one as before, wide open. You got a latch loose or something?"

Tyler rubbed his temple. "No, sir."

"Didn't see any damage or animals roaming about where they shouldn't be, but still. It concerns me to think some joy-riding teenagers are using your mama's land for their playground."

What made him think immediately of high schoolers?

The timing of Uncle Jed's call didn't sit right with Tyler. Seemed a bit convenient he'd notice the opened gate now, not even two hours after the youth group's excursion. Could be one of them had acted unruly, although that would mean at least three different customers on three different occasions had trespassed onto his mom's farm. That seemed an unlikely percentage.

If anything, today's incident only strengthened his suspicion that a local youth was to blame.

He'd check the camera tonight.

Chapter Thirteen

Nolan darted from the car to the sidewalk, cutting off a woman with a toddler before Daria had a chance to stop him. "Wait, please." Standing beside Isla's opened door, the child fighting to break free from her car seat, she shot her nephew a stern look.

She eyed the parked vehicles for Tyler's truck, and a smile formed unbidden when she spotted it. Not many men would choose to spend their afternoon at a preschool event. Yet, here he was, remaining present in her and the children's lives.

He'd make a wonderful husband and father, and she was beginning to think, or at least hope, that he'd choose to stay in Sage Creek with her and the kids.

She unfastened Isla, grabbed her diaper bag, and met Nolan outside the bookstore's single door. Inside, the aroma of fresh brewed coffee and baked goods filled the air. Southern gospel played softly from unseen speakers. A few professionals dressed in business attire were interspersed among moms and children, some in gym clothes, others in trendy outfits. Daria recognized some of them from church but didn't know them well enough to initiate conversation.

She probably needed to make more of an effort to form relationships. Yet, between Lucy and Ann, her friend bucket felt pleasantly full. God had so graciously provided for Daria's needs, replacing her fear of abandonment and the loneliness that had characterized her life in Illinois with a sense of belonging and the fulfillment of being known.

Nolan tugged his hand free from hers and dashed straight to the bakery case. He pressed his nose to the glass, his face framed by his hands. Isla struggled to get down. The moment Daria set her niece on her feet, she toddled to her brother.

Scanning the crowd for a glimpse of Tyler, Daria filed in line behind a tall woman with short blond hair and bony shoulders.

"Daria, hello."

She turned to see Gabrielle, a Realtor she'd spoken with briefly when she first moved to Sage Creek, approaching her with a large smile. "Hi."

"Last we met, I told you I'd let you know if any land close to yours came available."

"I appreciate that. Unfortunately, I don't think I'll be able to expand my property for some time." If ever. Although her outlook could change if she continued to have days like today. She needed to target as many larger groups as possible. From the church, the camp run by Elias, maybe even market her services as a team-building opportunity for local businesses.

"I imagine you've just gotten settled where you're at," Gabrielle said. "Still, you might want to keep the expansion door open, this being a buyer's market and all."

It wouldn't hurt to hear her options. Who knew, maybe God would decide to bless her business to the point that she could afford additional acreage. "Do you know of a place for sale?"

"Not yet, but soon, and right next to yours." She grinned. "The Reyeses' property. If you jump on it now before they list it, I'm confident you can snag it for a phe-nomenal price."

Daria blinked. "Ann is planning to sell?" She knew things had been tight, but she'd never imagined her friend's finances were bad enough to warrant such a deci-sion. She could understand how downsizing might make it easier for her friend to manage her farm, but wouldn't that cut into her profits as well? "How many acres?"

"All of it, although she might be willing to split up her land. If interested, I suggest you move fast. Her son wants the property sold quickly so he can get his mom moved out and settled with him in Omaha."

Her stomach sank. She knew Tyler was planning on leaving, although she'd hoped he'd change his mind. But Ann, too? She'd lose a dear friend and a major source of emotional support because of him. Daria doubted Ann would've considered such a thing otherwise.

Tyler knew how much his mom meant to her and the children. And he hadn't had the decency to tell her? Seemed he was just like all the others who'd popped into her life long enough to break through her defenses before slipping out with little more than a goodbye.

Gabrielle's phone rang. She pulled it from her purse's side pocket, glanced at the screen, and then excused her-self to take it.

Turning back to the line of people in front of her, Daria inched forward as a familiar emptiness she'd felt often as a kid swept over her.

She would not cry. Not here, and not now.

Inhaling, she focused on the menu, reading it item by

item until the threat of tears had passed. Once it was her turn, she asked for two kid-sized chocolate milks and a monster cookie for Nolan and Isla to share. Although she'd lost her appetite, she ordered an iced mocha and a slice of apple spiced bread for herself.

With Isla and Nolan accompanying her, she carried their treats to the kids' section at the back of the store. Numerous mothers and children already filled the space. Some sat on the long benches arranged end to end to form half a hexagon in front of the stage while others occupied the section of floor between.

Nodding hello to the few ladies she knew, she wove around mothers and wiggly preschoolers to an alcove seating area along the far wall. She didn't look behind her or about to see if Tyler had ambled in. Should he spy her, she hoped the room full of women would deter him from making his way to her. She realized she couldn't avoid him forever, but she could at least give herself time to process what she'd just learned.

He approached her when they transitioned to craft time. "Hey there." He grinned.

A lump lodged in her throat. "Hi." Handing Isla a small tube of glitter glue, she focused on the construction paper in front of her to hide her pain.

Nolan squeezed a massive glob onto his page. She placed a gentle hand over his and gave him a craft stick. "That's enough. Now spread it around like this." She demonstrated. She sensed Tyler studying her as she continued guiding both children in completing their projects.

Isla held out a marker. "Hewp?"

Tyler took it and leaned in closer. "Want me to draw something?"

She nodded.

"Like what? Clouds?"

"Yes." She pointed to the bottom of her page.

"Right there?"

She nodded and pointed again, first on the right, then left, then dead center.

"Your wish is my command, darling." He flashed Daria a grin that soon turned to a look of concern. "You all right?"

"Just thinking through some things."

"About work?"

"I'm fine." This wasn't anything she wanted to talk about now. She worried her emotions were so close to the surface that she'd start to cry if he kept pestering her. "How was your afternoon?" She wasn't in the mood for chitchat, but small talk felt safer. "Were you able to get much work done on the farm?" She hoped he didn't notice the quiver in her voice.

"Had the farrier out to check a shifted shoe, worked on my mom's vehicle some, then I called around to a few junkyards to see about purchasing a used transmission." This led to a story about a time during his elementary years when his dad decided he wanted to fix up old beater cars. "Might not have been a bad hobby, if he'd finished what he started. In the end, all he had to show for his efforts was a bunch of rusted metal to add to all the other items stored and forgotten in the barn of disarray."

He followed this with a story about a time when, also during his younger days, he ran away and spent a week sleeping in the hayloft. She responded with an occasional question or mmm-hmm to let him know she was listening, but her mind remained stuck on her conversation with the Realtor and the gaping hole his and Ann's move would leave in her and the children's lives.

When the children's event ended, people stood. Some gathered to talk in groups of three and four, others perused the shelves, and still others streamed out. As Daria and the children were leaving, Nolan was sidelined by a dinosaur encyclopedia left on a table.

He turned to Tyler. "Will you read this to me?"

He glanced at his phone screen. "Sorry, bud, but I best be getting back so I can tend to my chores before dinner with your auntie."

Nolan scowled, arms crossed. "You never want to be with me."

"That's not true." Tyler reached a hand to the child's shoulder, but Nolan jerked away and positioned himself on Daria's other side.

It saddened her to see Nolan's anger resurface, and just when it had seemed as if his heart was beginning to heal. She knew grief could hit a person in powerful, unexpected ways. It pained her to think her nephew's sorrow would only intensify once Tyler and his mom left.

Tyler halted as they were heading out. "I can pick you up at seven. That work?"

A deep ache seized her chest. "I'm sorry, but I'm not going to be able to make it."

Lines etched across his forehead. "Tomorrow, then?"

"I'll let you know."

The confusion in his eyes intensified the ache she felt. She didn't want to hurt him, which was why she needed to give herself time to process the emotions raging within her. To gain God's perspective, comfort, and guidance.

She'd experienced the wreckage that came from speaking from a place of unresolved pain.

That night, unable to sleep, she made herself a mug of citrus chamomile tea and took it, along with her Bible and journal, to the back porch table. Crickets chirped, and a bullfrog croaked from somewhere behind her. Casting the yard in a silver glow, the waning moon looked exceptionally bright against a clear sky.

Closing her eyes, she thought of the night Tyler had taken her riding. The tenderness in his eyes as he'd helped her onto the horse and then waited for her to grow comfortable on such a powerful animal had nearly stolen her breath. The night had been so peaceful, the sounds of crickets and rhythmic hooves thumping across the pasture the only noise. In that moment, it had felt as if the world had shrunk to just the two of them.

She'd felt certain he shared her reluctance to return to the farmhouse. That perhaps, like her, he was beginning to think in terms of forever.

Either she'd misread him, or he'd considered their relationship and chosen differently. Was that why he'd asked her to dinner? So that he could tell her, without the kids present, that he was leaving with his mom?

Her throat burned as she fought a wave of tears.

Had she really thought that he would adjust his life for her? No one else in her life, other than Lucy, had ever done that. She'd walked straight into this pain fully cognizant of where things were headed. But she'd spent so much time denying reality that she'd come to believe that her relationship with Tyler would end differently than those she'd formed in the past.

That it wouldn't end at all.

What made this even harder was knowing that she'd dragged her niece and nephew along with her.

Was this what people meant when they said love was blind?

The sliding glass door squeaked open, and Lucy stepped out wearing polka-dotted pajama shorts and a pink T-shirt. She looked at Daria for a moment and then took the chair across from her. "Can't sleep?"

Daria shook her head, worried if she spoke, she'd cry.

Lucy waited, her eyes radiating compassion.

After a few deep breaths, Daria shared the conversation she'd had with Gabrielle and why it hurt so deeply.

"I'm sorry, sweetie." Lucy took Daria's hand in hers.

She palmed away a tear slipping down her cheek. "I know I don't have any right to be upset. It's not like he said he loved me or even promised me anything."

"What are you feeling in your body?"

Lucy had asked Daria that question numerous times back when she was a kid trying to process hard experiences related to growing up as a foster kid.

Daria paused to process her physical sensations. "I feel nauseous. Like there's an emptiness in my gut."

"When have you felt this before?"

"Whenever the state moved me to a new placement."

"And the first time?"

"When the social worker came to take my sister and me from my mom." She couldn't remember how old she'd been. So much of her childhood, especially in those early years, remained a blur, with images flashing here and there. But she did remember that woman—Samantha. The color of her hair, the sound of her voice, even what she'd worn that day. Blue slacks, a white blouse, and a small black watch. "Then again a couple years later when my court-appointed advocate testified against my mom and she lost her parental rights for good."

Her name was Morgan, and she'd been a short, plump woman in her midforties with long brown hair streaked with gray. Daria hadn't been sure how she felt about Morgan when they first met. Knowing she was court-assigned, Daria lumped her with everyone else who seemed bent on ruining her life. But over time and lots of ice cream outings, Morgan had earned her trust.

Daria had come to believe that the woman truly cared about her.

She gazed across the yard without focusing on anything. "I felt so betrayed. I know it wasn't her fault my mom lost us, but back then, I blamed her."

"Are you doing the same with Tyler now?"

"Maybe."

"Which only makes your pain all the more intense."

She nodded.

Lucy leaned forward, eyes locked on Daria's. "You know what that means, right?"

She shook her head.

"I know you're sad about Tyler, and understandably so. But the fact that all of this is stirring up so much from your past means God wants to bring you to a new level of healing. And freedom. So that when the right man comes along, you'll be able to embrace that relationship without fear."

"But I thought Tyler was the right man." Couldn't God mend her heart without breaking it first? And without taking from her the only man she'd ever envisioned spending the rest of her life with?

"Do you trust God?"

Daria swallowed and squeezed her eyes shut. "I want to."

Help me to trust You, Lord, to know that one day You'll replace my grief with joy.

The next morning, Tyler woke early, grabbed a quick shower and bite to eat. With a steaming mug of coffee and blueberry muffin in hand and hunting camera under his arm, he headed straight for the guest room his mom used as an office.

He'd meant to check the footage the night before but

had gotten sidetracked dealing with an injured horse. It didn't help that the vet had been tied up with another emergency on someone's ranch. The rest of the night, he'd tossed and turned, worrying about Daria. He could tell something had happened. With the children or Lucy? Her business? Whatever it was, he knew God would carry her through.

He turned on the camera, rewound the SD card, and hit rapid playback. Two hours' worth of footage in, he blinked.

Uncle Jed parked, stepped out of his truck, glanced about, and kicked one of the posts Tyler had replaced. Clearly frustrated when it didn't budge, he spit onto the ground, threw open the gate, and pulled out his phone.

He checked the time stamp on the recording. That was right before Uncle Jed had called Tyler. But that didn't make sense.

Yet, it did. Hadn't Tyler heard Jed was hoping to expand his farm? But the man was a longtime friend.

Of Tyler's father.

He'd either taken sides in the divorce or his loyalty had never extended to Tyler's mom. Or greed and opportunity had obliterated whatever goodwill he'd once held for their family.

Tyler's jaw clenched as he thought of all the words he'd like to say to the man the next time he saw him. He wanted to tell him just what a low-life loser he thought he was for targeting two single women like he had. All while pretending to have his mom's best interests in mind.

That was why he knew he'd be better off sending an email with the video attached to avoid any ambiguity, confusion, or need for conversation.

Tyler might not maintain self-control otherwise.

He slipped the SD card into his mom's laptop, prayed

for the Holy Spirit to overpower his desire to type out an ugly message, and then shifted his focus to why he'd come into his mom's office in the first place.

If he was going to turn this place around and build a future for Daria, the kids, and himself, he needed to know exactly what he was up against. Although his mom had never said, he feared she carried sizable debt.

Her desk was covered with mail, invoices, and various seed catalogs. He sat in her squeaky wooden chair and began sorting through her clutter. This wasn't helping. In order to get a feel for where she stood, he needed to see her bank statements.

He glanced at the computer screen. The file had loaded. He paused with his hands over the keyboard, knowing his next sentence might not be the most Christlike he could offer, but the man had tried to hurt his mom. Jed needed to know the seriousness of his actions.

Teeth clenched, he typed, You're lucky we're not pressing charges, and hit Send.

That would keep the lying cheat from sabotaging his mom's—or Daria's—source of livelihood.

He turned to the waist-high, canary-yellow filing cabinet standing in the closet and resumed his search through his mom's documents. What he found made him ill. Sinking back into her chair, he dropped his head into his hands. He glanced at the clock on the wall. She'd be up soon, if she wasn't already.

After a few deep breaths and a quick prayer for guidance, he exited the room to speak with her. He found her at the kitchen stove. The smell of bacon and melted butter filled the space.

She glanced over her shoulder with a warm smile. "Good morning. Hungry?"

"Not really." His gut felt too knotted for food.

He studied her, greeted her with a kiss to the cheek, and sat at the table. Hopefully, his brother wouldn't break his habit of sleeping in. This wasn't a conversation Tyler wanted to invite Wesley into. He'd probably only added to this mess.

His mom set a plate with bacon, grits, and scrambled eggs in front of him, returned for her orange juice and a banana, then sat across from him. "Sleep well?"

"All right." Hands in his lap, he rubbed his thumb knuckle. "When did you refinance the farm?"

Her eyes widened. Dropping her gaze, she focused on unpeeling her banana. "A while ago."

"You're underwater. Is that why you don't want to sell?" How could she, when she owed more than she'd get for it.

"I'll be able to pay that off soon."

"How? Because I know you didn't make enough from the wheat harvest."

"I made an investment."

His stomach dropped. "What kind of investment?"

"In a cryptocurrency company your brother learned about."

The air expelled from his lungs. "Tell me you didn't buy into one of Wesley's get-rich-quick ideas."

"This is with a legitimate company. I've already made a profit."

"That's not what your bank statement shows."

She lifted her chin. "Why were you going through my records?"

Footsteps approached from behind and then stopped. He turned to see Wesley standing in the kitchen entrance, hair mussed, posture stiff.

Of all mornings for him to rise early. Then again, he needed to hear this. To help fix this.

He faced his mom once again. "I needed to know where you stood so I could gauge what we're up against." He rubbed his face. Putting her on the defensive wouldn't help matters. "You've seen a return on your investment?"

She nodded. "I was up twenty percent. I saw the reports myself." She looked at her youngest with a pleading expression. "Tell him, Wesley."

Tyler's brother seemed to struggle to maintain eye contact.

When he didn't reply, their mom continued, "I knew this was how I'd save the farm, so when I had an opportunity to invest more, I did."

"Using funds from where? Your increase?"

She nodded.

"And?"

"Equity from our house and land."

"Mom, you need to call whomever you're dealing with and tell them you want out. As soon as possible."

She looked at Wesley, who remained frozen where he was, arms tightly crossed.

"Well?" Tyler fought to remain calm.

Wesley's Adam's apple dipped. "I've been trying to get ahold of him."

"Let me guess. His number's been disconnected."

Rubbing his wrist, Wesley's gaze dropped to the floor and then past Tyler. He gave a barely visible shrug.

"I'm sure there's an explanation." The lines across their mom's forehead deepened. "The man seemed so nice, and I saw the numbers myself." Her voice cracked. "You don't think…" Moisture shined in her eyes.

He reached across the table and placed a hand over hers. "I hate to say this, but I fear you've been conned."

She made a sobbing noise as tears slid down her cheeks. "Are you sure?"

He nodded. He'd learned a long time ago that if something seemed too good to be true, it most likely was—investment schemes especially.

"Now what?"

Tyler looked at his brother, who seemed to shrink. A heavy silence filled the room.

Wesley walked to the table and sank into a chair kitty-corner to their mom. Rubbing his temples, eyes down, he shook his head. "This is all my fault. I should have known. I was trying to help."

Their mom reached for his hand, tears building behind her lashes. "I know, son. I appreciate that."

The tendons in Tyler's neck stretched taut. "Were you? Or were you using Mom's money for yet another one of your schemes?"

Wesley winced.

"That's enough." Their mom's voice was low but firm. "He knows he made a mistake. We'll deal with it."

Tyler could feel his temperature rising and knew he needed to hit pause. To breathe. But he'd about had enough of his brother causing his mom pain. "How many times are you going to make Mom clean up after your messes, huh?"

Wesley shook his head, more forcefully this time. "I'll file charges. The authorities can find the guy and get our money back."

Tyler huffed. "Don't count on that. Most likely, the schmuck's spent every dime and bailed."

"I'll take care of this," Wesley said.

"Yeah? And how's that?"

"I'll figure it out." His voice sounded strangled. "I'll get a job to pay her back. And I'll help more around the farm."

Like he should've been doing all along. Not that Tyler

had room to talk on that account. If he'd been here, the farm wouldn't have fallen apart, and maybe his dad would never have left. Then his mom wouldn't have landed in this hole.

"What if the bank forecloses on the property?" Her words came out on a sob.

"We won't let that happen." Tyler had money left in his savings. Not enough to cover it all, but with that, a few strong harvests, and frugal living, they could pay it off. Especially if Wesley helped like he promised.

Tyler intended to hold him to that.

"How can you stop them?" The desperation stabbed at Tyler's heart.

"Together—" he stressed the word and narrowed his gaze onto his brother "—we're going to turn this place around. No matter how long that takes."

"You mean...?" Her bottom lip started to quiver.

Tyler squared his shoulders. "I mean I'm staying. For good."

"Oh, Tyler. Thank you!" Palm to her chest, her voice cracked.

He nodded. "Now, if you'll excuse me, I need to think this through."

He had to process what all this meant, not just in terms of the uphill climb ahead of them, but how all this would affect Daria and the children as well.

He stood, rounded the table to give his mom a hug, and then left for an early morning horse ride.

When he reached the end of his mom's property, he turned left and continued down a long, gravel road and across railroad tracks bordering a stretch of meadow splattered with wildflowers.

Beyond this, an old wooden bridge stretched across a stream that swelled each spring.

This had been one of his favorite thinking spots as a kid. It was far enough out to burn away whatever agitated energy had driven him to the stables. Far enough, also, that no one would find him, even if they went looking.

There was something about sitting here gazing up at the endless sky, grass tufts tickling his bare elbows, that helped him make sense of his thoughts. And this morning, he had plenty to untangle.

If he turned things around and saved the farm, Daria could use whatever pasture they left fallow each year for an archery range, with a tractor-pulled hayride to get guests there. His mom could hold on to the way of life she loved. And God willing, Tyler could keep the woman he loved.

So long as Daria felt the same. He knew God was leading him to pursue a future with her, but if she wasn't interested, he needed to let her go, as much as that would hurt. There was so much at stake, for her and the kids.

He longed to give her the world, not strap her to a lifetime of financial insecurity.

He loved her so much it hurt. More than he'd ever loved a woman, if indeed he ever had prior. *Lord, give me wisdom here. And give me the strength to do what's best for them, even if that means releasing the woman I love.*

Words from a familiar Bible verse came to mind. "Delight thyself also in the Lord: and he shall give thee the desires of thine heart."

Father, I'm taking that as a promise.

He checked the time on his phone. Just after 8:00 a.m., late enough that his buddy in Omaha would be awake.

Still sitting in his saddle, he called.

"Hey." His friend's tone carried warmth. "How's the move coming? Need me to help you lift the heavies?"

Although confident of God's guidance, he couldn't

help but feel like he was choosing between honoring his friend, and caring for his mom, and building a lasting relationship with Daria and the children.

He released a breath. "I really appreciate you providing me with an in with the railroad. And I know how much a man's word means. That you put your name on the line for me."

"No big deal. They're lucky to have you."

"About that. I'm going to have to decline the job offer."

There was a moment of silence before his friend spoke again. "Is your mom okay?"

He'd told his friend about the divorce and his concerns regarding the farm. "She will be. But I've decided to stay."

"I admire that, bro."

"Thanks. I'm just sorry for how my decision will affect you."

"Don't be. Actually, I was going to call you once the ink dried on my relocation contract. I'm leaving the company."

"Seriously? When? Why?"

"A headhunter for a consulting firm reached out to me and made me an offer I couldn't refuse."

Pastor Roger often said when a person obeyed Jesus, He took care of everything else. The fact that He'd done so in relation to the job helped Tyler trust that God would manage the other details of his life as well, those related to Daria included.

Chapter Fourteen

Daria dashed over to Ann's early the next morning before church to help with last minute preparations for the flea market. She brought the children with her. She loved the way her friend included Nolan in each step of the process. Not only did this make him feel valued, but it provided a great education in entrepreneurship as well.

It also deepened the bond that would ultimately lead her nephew to increased grief. But Daria couldn't think about that now, not if she wanted to get through her day without breaking into tears.

She picked up a box full of antique, textured-glass dishes. "Nolan, can you come open the car door for me?"

Nodding, he sprang to his feet and dashed outside and onto the porch ahead of her. There, he halted, and his posture stiffened before he continued to the car.

Daria turned to see Tyler approaching from the stables.

He reached them as she was depositing her load onto the passenger side's floorboard. "Hey." He grinned, looking first to Daria and then to Nolan. "If it isn't my favorite cowboy. Where's your hat?"

Nolan touched his head, as if he'd forgotten whether

or not he'd placed anything on it, and frowned. "I don't like it."

Lines stretched across Tyler's forehead. "Okay." Hand on his belt buckle, he shifted toward Daria. "You two up for more riding tonight?"

She took in a deep breath. She had no business being angry at Tyler. He'd never made her any promises, and she knew he only wanted what was best for his mom. Clearly, he felt that was moving her to Omaha, which made sense. Ann couldn't manage this farm on her own.

The question was, could she emotionally handle spending another evening with him, having fully opened her heart, knowing it would soon break?

Would she regret not spending time with him when she had the opportunity to do so?

She faced Nolan. "What do you think, kiddo? You up for another lesson?"

"No." He darted past her and into the house.

Daria blinked. What was that about? Was he sensing and reacting to her sorrow? If so, she needed to be more careful.

She turned to Tyler. "Maybe another time." Not that they had much of that remaining.

"Sure." He followed her into the living room and surveyed the items retrieved from the junk barn. "I can help."

His mom straightened and swiped her hair out of her face with her forearm. "If you've got time, that would be lovely."

He nodded and reached for a vase and some wrapping tissue. "I can spare an hour or so."

Daria tried to engage while he made chitchat, but her smile felt stiff. She could tell by the way Tyler cast frequent glances her way that he was concerned, but he didn't say anything. Not until they'd loaded everything into one of their three vehicles.

He closed his pickup's tailgate and turned toward her. "Wanted to let you know, I got to the bottom of the vandalism issue. Turns out one of my dad's old friends was trying to sabotage you and my mom."

"Why?"

He shrugged. "Probably hoping you'd both want to sell and he could buy cheap." The man had responded to Tyler's email with a wordy excuse about how he'd been wanting to help his mom realize how challenging her situation was, so that she'd get out from under the farm. But Tyler wasn't buying it.

"That's terrible. But I'm glad you got it figured out."

He nodded, studying her. "You seem sad. Is everything all right?"

The compassion in his eyes tore at her already bruised heart. She nodded. "Just processing some things."

He studied her a moment longer and then nodded. "I imagine you've got to get back to work, but if you need a listening ear, I'd love to take you out for dessert after."

"I appreciate the offer, but I'll be fine." And she would be, eventually. She'd endured enough pain in her life to know that. Except she'd never loved before. Not like this.

The house door squeaked open as Nolan barreled out.

Ann followed carrying Isla. "Mind if I snag the children for the rest of the morning? They want to see Oreo and the goats. I can bring them to you after lunch."

"You don't need—"

"Hush, now." The humor in her eyes contradicted her stern expression. "You know nothing would make me happier than spending time with these two."

Daria's eyes stung with the threat of tears. Although being here now hurt, she was thankful for every moment the children got to spend with the sweet woman. "If you insist."

"I do." With a quick nod, Ann strode after Nolan, who'd already skipped halfway to the hay barn.

Daria watched them leave then turned to Tyler. "I best get to work. I've got a group coming in at eleven." She'd hoped to ask Ann about her selling the farm but hadn't managed to catch the woman alone away from Nolan's alert ears. That was probably for the best, as such a discussion would only have made Daria cry.

Maybe that was why Ann had never broached the subject with her. This was probably as hard for her as it was for Daria, if not more so. Her husband had left, and now she was going to be relinquishing the farm she loved and would have to say goodbye to the children. Daria knew how much Ann loved them—all of them.

Would she come back to visit? What about Tyler? Could Daria even handle that? It was one thing to maintain a long-distance relationship with a friend. It would be much more painful trying to do so with the man she loved, especially if he fell in love with someone else in Omaha.

And he would. She'd be a fool to think otherwise.

"You're taking tomorrow off?" Tyler asked.

She nodded.

He walked her to her car and held her door open for her. "Guess I'll see you then. Although remember, the offer for dessert still stands, for tonight, tomorrow night, or the night after. For whenever you want to talk."

Did he always have to be so…perfect?

She sucked in a quick breath and slid behind the steering wheel. "I appreciate that." The rest of the day, she stayed busy, if not with customers, then with decluttering her office and organizing her workshop—anything to keep her emotions in check.

Unfortunately, they hit her with full force the moment her head met her pillow that night. She was happy for Ann and Tyler, she truly was. Everyone needed family to lean on during difficult times. Whether they lived together or simply in the same city, Tyler would take great care of his mom, of that Daria was certain. And Ann would take care of Tyler in her own way—which would definitely involve baked goods of some sort.

How could she soften the blow for Nolan? Despite how aloof he'd behaved toward Tyler this morning, she knew he adored both Tyler and his mom.

"Lord, I know somehow, someday, You'll turn all this to good for everyone involved, because that's what the Bible promises. Help me to hold tight to that truth, knowing our pain won't last forever. I choose to trust You, despite how badly this hurts now. And thank You for the time You've allowed the children and I to spend with Ann and Tyler, two people I will always cherish."

Perhaps her ability to say that, even with a breaking heart, indicated how far she'd come. She'd not only let Tyler in, but she'd resisted the urge to respond to the pain by withdrawing and shutting down.

During church, the pastor gave a sermon on holding tight to God's promises while walking through difficult valleys. In her Bible, she found and underlined the verse he quoted. It was from Psalm 30:5 and said, "Weeping may endure for a night, but joy cometh in the morning."

While this didn't lessen her heartache, it did remind her that her pain wouldn't last forever.

Just over an hour later, she met Ann and Tyler on Main Street to help set up for the antiques fair. Over half of the other vendors had already arrived. She assumed the latecomers had chosen to attend church first, as she had. She knew Ann had wanted to arrive first thing, but she'd been gracious enough to wait on Daria and the kids.

Once she, Ann, and Tyler had unloaded their boxes and arranged their contents, Tyler offered to stay with the children while Ann and Daria moved their vehicles. "I'm in no hurry."

Ann rearranged three matching votive candles on the table. "You planning on sticking around today?"

He nodded. "I need to take care of something first, but yeah."

"Thank you." Daria smiled. "I'll be quick."

Nolan scurried after her. "I want to come."

"Sweetie, I'm just going to park. Then I'll have to walk back. I'm not sure how far."

"So?" He crossed his arms.

What was up with him? She would've thought he'd jump at the chance to spend time with Tyler. First, he'd refused to wear his cowboy hat, then he didn't want to go riding, and now this. Had he overheard Ann and Tyler talking about their plans to move? Maybe after she'd left for work yesterday morning?

If so, that would've been a heavy blow. Yet two more people he would need to grieve.

She exhaled. "Okay." She let Isla stay with Tyler, who had found her play phone and was engaging her in a simple, mock conversation.

Nolan followed her to the car and climbed into his booster seat while she held his door. Once he was fastened in, she slid behind the wheel and followed a man with a truck pulling a small cargo trailer to the designated parking behind city hall.

Unfortunately, others had already taken all the shaded spaces. She eased her vehicle between a silver hatchback and a heavily dented minivan, pulled Nolan's feeling chart from the glovebox, and handed it to him.

"Here, buddy." She made eye contact with her nephew through the rearview mirror. "Can you let me know which face most shows how you're feeling?"

According to her former therapist, simply naming an emotion helped to reduce its intensity. With children, it also increased their self-awareness and made it easier for them to talk about whatever they were experiencing internally.

At least, that was her goal.

Concentration lines stretched across his forehead as he studied the pictures. "This." He tapped an angry face. "And this one." He touched the sad face.

"You feel angry and sad?"

He nodded. "You're *my* friend."

"I'm your aunt, and I love you very much."

"But you're mine."

Where was this coming from? Was he battling sibling rivalry? Except he'd seemed fine when she'd engaged with Isla this morning. Maybe he was experiencing a fear of abandonment. That would make sense after having lost his mom. "Are you afraid I'll leave you?"

He dropped the chart and stuck the tail of his dinosaur into his mouth.

She placed a hand on his knee. "Sweetie, you're safe. I'm not going anywhere. Want to snuggle for a minute?"

Tears building in his eyes, he nodded and unclicked his booster seat straps.

Seat belt unfastened, she maneuvered over the center console to the passenger's side and helped him climb into the front and onto her lap. With his cheek resting against her chest, head tucked beneath her chin, she rubbed his back while softly singing. "You're my Nolan, my precious Nolan, and I am here, when your world feels gray. I will hold you, I will love you, and my love will always be here to stay."

If only her love could shield him from the pain she knew he'd soon experience once Ann and Tyler left.

When Tyler's mom returned, she thanked him for keeping an eye on the little one and their stuff. She sat in one of the folding chairs arranged behind her and Nolan's tables, pulled a bubbles container from her tote, and opened it.

"Come sit with Nana Ann." She softly blew through the wand.

Isla abandoned the sensory cube she'd been playing with and scrambled up into the seat next to his mom. "Again."

Ann complied, sending iridescent bubbles of various sizes into the air. One landed on Isla's nose.

The child squealed. "Again."

Tyler glanced down the street, surveying the sea of heads and booth umbrellas for a glimpse of Daria. Depending on how cooperative or distractible Nolan was, she could be a while.

He kissed the top of Isla's head and looked at his mom. "You okay if I go?"

"Sure, abandon us." She waved a hand, laughter gleaming in her eyes.

"Thanks." He gave her a side hug and left.

Ten minutes later, truck parked, he walked down Main Street past the Literary Sweet Spot. The aroma of fresh baked goods merged with the scent of candied nuts and caramel popcorn emanating from a street vendor's aluminum tumbler. Country music drifted from one of the nearby stores, Southern gospel from another.

The Blue Bonnet Boutique had brought out two racks

of discounted clothes, a few hand-painted pieces of furniture, and a shelf on wheels holding mugs, plaques, and decorative magnets to the sidewalk. A bell above the door chimed as he entered, and a blast of cold air swept over him.

"My word." Yolanda, the owner, stepped out from behind the cash register and display case. "If it isn't Tyler Reyes. I heard you were back in town."

"Ma'am." He tipped his hat and glanced about.

"Who are you shopping for?"

"Uh… I was hoping to look at your jewelry."

"Follow me." She led the way around a table of folded T-shirts, past a rotating metal rack of greeting cards, to an array of fine jewelry in the back corner.

Odd that she'd placed her most expensive items here, where most folks might never see them. Then again, the majority of her customers probably came for knickknacks and whatnot. Those, like him, wanting to purchase engagement rings, either knew where to go or would ask for help.

He explained why he'd come.

Smiling, she clasped her hands together under her chin. "How exciting." She moved behind the glass-encased shelf. "As you can see, we have numerous designs to choose from." She plucked one made from white gold with a square center diamond. "This princess baguette with a pavé setting is one of our most popular. Total diamond weight is a half carat."

Eyeing the piece, he rubbed the back of his hand under his chin. "That's beautiful, but I'm not sure it matches her style."

"Something with more bling, perhaps?"

She returned the first ring and reached for another

over double the price. It had a much larger center diamond and more stones set in the band.

"Not that one." Her words from the day she'd told him
about her bracelet came to mind. *I don't even like jewelry much.* "Do you have anything…more understated?"
He really should've brought his mom with him for this.

Yolanda showed him a few more pieces, but none of
them felt quite right, although his hesitation could just
as easily come from nerves.

He stepped back. "Mind if I think on this?"

She smiled. "Absolutely. Take all the time you need."

Unfortunately, Yolanda's was the only jewelry store
in town, unless one counted the secondhand store farther down. He might need to try somewhere in Houston.

He thanked Yolanda for her help and headed back the
way he'd come. As he passed the secondhand store, a
round gem in a simple gold band caught his eye. If displayed elsewhere, he'd say it was perfect, but should he
really buy Daria a used engagement ring? Something
about it felt right.

Casting a glance toward the blue sky disrupted by
the occasional cotton-ball cloud, he entered the dim and
dusty store. "Lord, I'm trusting You to guide me, because
I really don't want to mess this up."

The sense of peace that followed assured him this indeed was Daria's ring.

"Hello." A middle-aged woman he didn't recognize
sat behind a long, cluttered counter. "Sure is a beautiful day, isn't it? I hear a storm might blow through on
Wednesday, but you know what they say about weather-
men. Their words have about as much substance as the
morning fog."

He laughed. "I haven't heard that one." He scratched

the back of his neck. "That ring in the window. Any way I can take a look at it?"

"Absolutely." She stepped around a mannequin wearing a black-and-white plaid dress suit and went to the front window to fetch the requested item. "This one has quite a story. Although passed down a couple generations, it was originally purchased by a soldier who fell head over heels for a young woman when he was stationed in France. Apparently, they fell in love almost immediately and began talking about dreams for their future. He was two years older and had obviously graduated from high school. She was sixteen with two more years to go. All too soon, it came time for his regiment to leave, but before they did, he took her for ice cream and to visit a jewelry store. He proposed to her that night and promised to come back for her."

"I'm guessing he didn't?"

She shook her head. "He was injured in combat and underwent a long recovery. By the time he returned to that little French village, the woman and her family had moved."

"That's so sad."

She nodded. "They reunited some twenty years later."

"Seriously? How?"

"The woman moved to the United States for college and eventually landed a job with a San Francisco newspaper. Lo and behold, one day the man picked up a paper left on a diner table. He started reading and saw her name. It was unique enough that it caught his attention. His logical side doubted the writer was the woman he loved, but his heart latched onto the possibility and wouldn't let go."

"He tracked her down?"

"Correct, with the engagement ring he'd purchased in his pocket. He'd kept it all that time for her."

"Wow. What a story."

"They were married for over forty years until the woman lost her battle with cancer. Story has it the man died from a broken heart less than six months later, and they've both been dancing the waltz in heaven ever since."

He grinned. "You sold me."

She smiled and led the way to the cash register. "If you and whoever you plan to give this to love one another the same way that couple did, I guarantee you'll have a long, happy marriage." She rang him up.

"I plan on it." He handed her his credit card and strolled back down the street with the ring in his pocket, thinking through when and how to pop the question.

His mom was gone when he returned to her and Nolan's booths. The little man was drawing on the asphalt with chalk while Isla napped in the shade of their umbrella. "Where's my mom?"

"She went to get us all something cold to drink," Daria said.

"That sounds amazing." He sat in the chair next to hers. "Y'all sell anything?"

"Some. Your mom got three hundred for the blue and green swirled vase."

"That's great." He looked at Nolan. "What about you, little man?"

Frowning, the boy shrugged.

Daria reached over and smoothed his bangs from his forehead. "He's made thirty dollars."

"Yeah!" Tyler held out a hand for a high five and then dropped it when Nolan frowned and looked away.

What had caused the little guy to act so surly lately?

A woman dressed like a clown passed by on an adult-sized tricycle. She'd attached balloon animals to her handlebars and had colorful flowers and vines painted on her face.

Stomach churning like it used to before giving a presentation in class, Tyler engaged Daria in small talk.

About fifteen minutes later, his mom returned with a drink tray holding three large lemonades and one small. She set this on the table and held a sweating cup out for Nolan. "Here you go, kiddo. So you're not 'about to catch fire,' as you say." She laughed and then looked at Tyler. "There's a guy near the end selling archery gear. Some bows and targets. Seemed like a great price. You should take Daria to go check them out."

Daria tore the wrapper off her straw. "I appreciate you thinking of me, but I don't want to leave you here on your own."

"Pretty sure I'll manage." She gave a teasing smile. "Besides, won't take you two but a minute. Now go, before someone snatches them up."

Tyler stood. "You know she won't quit pestering us until we do as she's asked, right?"

Daria smiled, but her eyes appeared sad. "Okay."

As they were about to leave, Nolan sprang to his feet. "No. You can't go." He grabbed her arm and tugged. "You have to play with me."

She blinked and seemed unsure how to respond. "Would you like to come with us?"

His scowl deepened. "Only you. Not him."

She lowered to the child's eye level. "I can tell you're upset, but that doesn't make it okay to be unkind. You and I can spend time together just the two of us later tonight. Okay?"

He shook his head. "No. Now." He pulled on her arm again. "Just me. Not him."

She took a deep breath, expression stern. "I love you,

and I understand it's hard to wait. But I need you to be patient. Mr. Tyler and I are going to go look at something. While we're gone, I expect you to behave."

"Don't talk to me." He took off running and disappeared among the throng of people before Tyler's brain caught up.

Tyler hurried after him, Daria close behind, both of them calling out to the child.

They stopped at the end of the block, out of breath.

"Where'd he go?" Daria's tone sounded panicked. "What if someone takes him? Or he gets lost?"

He placed a hand on her shoulder. "We'll find him. Most likely he darted into a store and is hiding under a clothing rack or something." He turned in a slow circle, scanning the crowded street and sidewalks, pushing down his fear so as not to alarm Daria further. "How about we split up? I'll go this way." He hooked a thumb eastward. "And you can go down there."

Eyes wide, she nodded and started back the way they'd come.

He headed in the opposite direction, asking numerous people if they'd seen a little boy just over three feet tall with wavy brown hair. He also gave out his number to call should they see him. His pulse accelerated with every no. Sage Creek was a safe town, but there were a lot of strangers and nonresidents that had come for the antiques fair.

Lord, please, help us find him. And keep him safe until we do.

He'd reached the bank and was about to turn down B Street when his phone rang. The fact that he didn't recognize the number sparked hope. Lungs tight, he answered. "Tyler Reyes."

"Hello. This is Mrs. Allcroft from church. You spoke

with me about twenty minutes ago, asked about that little boy?"

"Yes?"

"He's at my house, sitting in the yard. I tried to get him to come in, but he acted like he wanted to take off, so I let him be. I've got an eye on him now through my kitchen window."

"What's your address?"

She told him.

"I'm on my way." Jogging that direction, he called Daria and relayed the information.

"Oh, thank You, Jesus!" Her words came out in a sob. "I'm at the park now."

It'd probably take her a good fifteen minutes on foot. "I'm not far."

"You'll make sure he doesn't go anywhere?"

"I will."

"I am so thankful for you."

The way she said that made him feel like her hero, a role he'd spend the rest of his life pursuing, God willing.

Chapter Fifteen

He cut through the library's back parking lot, past a single-story house with wood siding and green trim to number 503. Mrs. Allcroft must have been watching for him, because she came out and met him at the end of her walk.

"He's over there, between my house and my neighbor's." She pointed.

"Thank you." Tyler crossed her lawn and rounded the corner to where Nolan sat in a diagonal patch of shade. "Hey, buddy."

Nolan looked up with a scowl. "Leave me alone."

He stood there for a moment, not sure how to respond. His gut told him the child needed him to do the opposite as he'd requested. To show he couldn't be pushed away that easily. The opposite, in fact—that he would pursue the boy, even when he acted out.

Tyler sat in the grass a few feet away, not saying anything.

After a while, Nolan glanced at him once again. "Why are you sitting there?"

Lord, give me the words he most needs to hear. "Because I think maybe you're sad, and I care about you."

"I don't like you."

"That's okay. I still care about you."

Nolan studied him, his pinched brow softening.

Tyler waited another moment. "Can I sit by you?"

He shrugged, so Tyler scooted closer. "Are you sad?"

"I'm mad."

Progress. "Okay. Do you know why?"

"Because you're not my friend. Not my auntie's friend, either. Uncuz she's my friend."

Oh. That's what this was about. "Buddy, I'm not going to take your aunt from you. She loves you more than the world, and she always will."

"But not you."

Could be the child was right, but Tyler hoped that wasn't the case. Regardless, that wasn't his primary concern right now. He needed to find a way to assure Nolan that his relationship with his aunt would remain secure, no matter who else she allowed into her life.

Tyler placed a hand on Nolan's. "I can't speak to how she feels about me," Tyler said. "But I know how I feel about you."

Nolan looked at him with a mixture of hurt and hope in his eyes.

"I love you, little man. And I want to be your friend, today, tomorrow, and for as long as you'll let me." That was a promise he intended to make good on, even if Daria refused his proposal.

"Tyler, you need to be honest with him."

He glanced up to see Daria standing a few feet away, her face downturned. "About?"

"You and your mom's plans to move."

How did she know about that? "We're not going anywhere."

Her frown deepened. "Then why did Gabrielle talk to me about buying your mom's property?"

He stood and moved toward her. "Originally, I intended to list it and talk my mom into coming with me to Omaha. But I changed my mind. I've decided to stay here in Sage Creek. With you."

"What are you saying?"

He hadn't planned on doing this today, but the time felt right. He patted his pocket, pulled out her engagement ring, and closed the distance between them. Dropping to one knee, he took her hand and opened the velvet jewelry box.

Palm on her chest, she gasped.

He swallowed, feeling so jittery he worried his words would tangle on his tongue. "Daria Ellis, I have never met a woman like you. So caring, strong, determined. I love watching you with the children. The tenderness that radiates from your eyes whenever they're near. I love the sound of your laugh and how your eyes dance when something amuses you. But mostly, I just love you. Everything about you. More than I ever knew I could love a person."

A tear slid down her cheek. "Oh, Tyler."

"I want to spend the rest of my life showing you just how much." His voice came out husky. He cleared his throat. "Doing all I can to be the man you—" he cast a glance behind him to Nolan, caught his eye, and winked "—and the kids deserve. If you and Nolan here will let me." He rotated so that he could see both the woman he adored and the child that had completely captured his heart. "What do you say, little man? Think you've got room in that family of yours to include a cowboy like me?"

"As my daddy?"

Hearing the child use that word to refer to him squeezed the air from his chest. "If you'll let me. What do you say?"

"Forever? You won't leave?"

Eyes stinging, Tyler shook his head. "I'm not going anywhere."

Nolan sprang to his feet, lunged toward Tyler, and slammed into him with a hug bearing the full force of his thirty-plus-pound frame. Holding him close with his free arm, Tyler kissed the child's head, breathing in the scent of little boy and the outdoors.

Nolan dropped his arms from around Tyler's neck and stepped back, looking at Daria. "Can he be my daddy?"

Tyler took a deep breath to steady his nerves. "Guess I should finish my question, huh?"

She nodded with a soggy laugh.

He cleared his throat. "Daria Ellis, will you make me the absolute happiest man alive by letting this cowboy stand by your side, in life's sunrises and sunsets, hailstorms and gentle spring rains. Forever, as your husband?"

"Yes!" She reached for him and fell into his open arms as he sprang to his feet. "I love you, Tyler Reyes."

Cupping her face in his hands, he studied her big brown eyes, noting every golden speck, every lash curl. "I'll never tire of hearing those words." His gaze dropped to her mouth, and he heard her breath hitch as he brushed his lips against hers, feathery soft at first, then growing in intensity as she melted against him.

His heart burned with the knowledge that he'd be holding her tightly for the rest of his life.

Epilogue

One year later

Tyler took a deep breath to calm his nerves. He still couldn't believe Daria had agreed to marry him. He was still trying to wrap his mind around the idea of spending the rest of his life with the woman he loved more than anything in the world.

Behind him stood a nineteenth-century shack decorated with translucent, cream drapes and centered with an arch made from thickly clustered roses. To his right, a string quartet made up of incredibly talented high school students, filled the air with their music.

The guests, sitting in the white folding chairs extended in front of him, gave a collective "Ah," as Nolan made his way down the aisle blowing bubbles and Isla darted this way and that in an attempt to capture the shimmering rainbows. Her giggles and bright-eyed wonder warmed his heart and elicited a sense of profound gratitude. This moment, this space, felt sacred, like a merging of heaven and earth.

But everything else faded from conscious thought when his bride emerged from around the corner and began walking toward him. She wore her amber-toned hair pulled back in a floral headband with wind-stirred whisps framing her face. Her lacey dress accentuated her trim figure. As she drew closer, he noticed the flush of her cheeks and the shimmer of unshed tears in her eyes.

She'd never looked more beautiful.

Taking her place beside him, she turned toward him with an almost shy smile. "Hey," she whispered.

"Hey," he whispered back, his thoughts halted on this one truth: this strong, tender, and courageous woman would soon be his, from this day forward, in good times and bad, until well after their hair turned gray.

Pastor Roger welcomed their guests and opened with a short reading from Scripture, followed by a poem Tyler and Daria had selected.

Then it was his turn. Hands clammy, he pulled a note-card from his pocket, shifted, and cleared his throat. "I'm not so great at putting words to how I feel. But I wanted to find a way to let you know how much you mean to me, even though that's impossible. There are just some things that can't be put into words, like the sunrise over a golden field, or a starry country sky."

He took a deep breath and continued. "Daria, in you, God fulfilled and ignited dreams I didn't know I had. Like laughing over a private joke no one else would find funny, if we tried to explain it. Or knowing, come tomorrow morning and a thousand after, your lovely face, with eyes that seem to see into my soul, will be the very first thing I see. Or anticipating lazy summer mornings sipping coffee on the porch or strolling, hand-in-hand across the pasture while the munchkins race ahead."

A tear slid down her cheek, and he thumbed it away. "But most importantly, knowing with you, the best is yet to come."

"Oh, Tyler, I love you so much."

"And I love you, more than I realized it was possible to love a person. So much my chest aches from the intensity of it. You will always steal my breath and hold my heart. From this day and forever beyond."

"And you, Tyler Reyes, will always have mine—without reservation."

A surge of emotion swept over him as he realized the depth of her words. She trusted him completely, and he knew trust didn't come easily for her.

His throat felt scratchy as his eyes locked onto hers. "I promise you this. Your heart will always be safe with me."

"Did you have vows you wanted to say, Daria?" Pastor Roger asked.

She sniffled, clearly fighting tears. "I'm not sure I can get the words out without turning into a blubbering mess, except to say that I know my heart is safe with you, Tyler, and I give it freely and fully."

The pastor instructed them to slip the rings on each other's fingers while declaring their commitment to one another. Then, tucking his Bible under his arm, he said, "I now pronounce you husband and wife." He clamped a hand on Tyler's shoulder. "You can now kiss your bride."

Tyler placed his hands on either side of her face and gently touched his lips to hers.

* * * * *

Dear Reader,

I once heard it said that a hurting child can survive and even grow up to thrive if they have one positive adult relationship in their lives. Daria Ellis is an example of this. She was born into generational abuse and dysfunction and could've easily followed in her mother's unhealthy and destructive footsteps. But she didn't because one woman named Lucy Carr took her in and showed her the consistent love that she needed. Because of this, she is now breaking the cycle of abuse and trauma in how she's raising her orphaned niece and nephew.

While Daria's story is just that, a story, there are many real women just like her and Lucy Carr—people who are acting as instruments of healing and those who've found the courage to break free from the chains that could otherwise create wreckage for generations to come. They chose—and choose—instead to create beauty and speak hope.

I love to connect with readers. You can reach out to me at jenniferaslattery@gmail.com, find me on Instagram at slatteryjennifer and on Facebook at Jennifer Slattery Author and Speaker.

Blessings,
Jennifer

CARING FOR HER AMISH NEIGHBOR
Amish of Prince Edward Island • by Jo Ann Brown

When an accident leaves Juan Kuepfer blind, widow Annalise Overgard and her daughter, who is visually impaired, are the only ones who can help. He needs to learn how to live without his sight, but being around them brings up guilt and grief from the past. Together can they find forgiveness and happiness?

HER HIDDEN AMISH CHILD
Secret Amish Babies • by Leigh Bale

Josiah Brenneman was heartbroken when his betrothed left town without a word. Now Faith Mast is back to sell her aunt's farm—with a *kind* in tow—and Josiah has questions. Why did she leave? Can he trust that she won't run away again? And who is the father of her child?

TO PROTECT HIS BROTHER'S BABY
Sundown Valley • by Linda Goodnight

Pregnant with nowhere to go, Taylor Matheson takes refuge at her late husband's ranch. Then Wilder Littlefield shows up, claiming the ranch is his. He can't evict his brother's widow, so she can stay until the baby arrives—but soon they start to feel like family...

THE COWBOY BARGAIN
Lazy M Ranch • by Tina Radcliffe

When Sam Morgan returns home from a business trip, he's stunned to discover his grandfather has rented the building Sam wanted to his former fiancée, Olivia Moretti. He's determined to keep his distance from the woman who broke his heart, but an Oklahoma twister changes his plans...

A FAMILY TO FOSTER
by Laurel Blount

Single dad Patrick Callahan will do anything to help the foster kids in his care—including saving Hope Center, a local spot for children from disadvantaged backgrounds. When his ex-fiancée, Torey Bryant, is named codirector by her matchmaking mom, it could spell disaster...or a second chance at love.

A FATHER FOR HER BOYS
by Danielle Grandinetti

Juggling a broken foot and guardianship of her nephews, Sofia Russo gladly takes a summer house-sitting gig out in the country. When they arrive, her boys are immediately taken with local landscaper Nathaniel Turner. And she can't help but feel something too. Could he be what they've been missing all along?

Get 3 FREE REWARDS!

We'll send you 2 FREE Books **plus** a FREE Mystery Gift.

FREE
Value Over
$20

Both the **Love Inspired** and **Love Inspired** Suspense series feature compelling novels filled with inspirational romance, faith, forgiveness and hope.

YES! Please send me 2 FREE novels from the Love Inspired or Love Inspired Suspense series and my FREE gift (gift is worth about $10 retail). After receiving them, if I don't wish to receive any more books, I can return the shipping statement marked "cancel." If I don't cancel, I will receive 6 brand-new Love Inspired Larger-Print books or Love Inspired Suspense Larger-Print books every month and be billed just $6.49 each in the U.S. or $6.74 each in Canada. That is a savings of at least 16% off the cover price. It's quite a bargain! Shipping and handling is just 50¢ per book in the U.S. and $1.25 per book in Canada.* I understand that accepting the 2 free books and gift places me under no obligation to buy anything. I can always return a shipment and cancel at any time by calling the number below. The free books and gift are mine to keep no matter what I decide.

Choose one: ☐ **Love Inspired**   ☐ **Love Inspired**   ☐ **Or Try Both!**
                   Larger-Print   **Suspense**   (122/322 & 107/307
                   (122/322 BPA GRPA)   **Larger-Print**   BPA GRRP)
                                                      (107/307 BPA GRPA)

_____

Name (please print)

_____

Address   Apt. #

_____

City   State/Province   Zip/Postal Code

Email: Please check this box ☐ if you would like to receive newsletters and promotional emails from Harlequin Enterprises ULC and its affiliates. You can unsubscribe anytime.

Mail to the **Harlequin Reader Service:**
IN U.S.A.: P.O. Box 1341, Buffalo, NY 14240-8531
IN CANADA: P.O. Box 603, Fort Erie, Ontario L2A 5X3

Want to try 2 free books from another series? Call 1-800-873-8635 or visit www.ReaderService.com.

*Terms and prices subject to change without notice. Prices do not include sales taxes, which will be charged (if applicable) based on your state or country of residence. Canadian residents will be charged applicable taxes. Offer not valid in Quebec. This offer is limited to one order per household. Books received may not be as shown. Not valid for current subscribers to the Love Inspired or Love Inspired Suspense series. All orders subject to approval. Credit or debit balances in a customer's account(s) may be offset by any other outstanding balance owed by or to the customer. Please allow 4 to 6 weeks for delivery. Offer available while quantities last.

Your Privacy—Your information is being collected by Harlequin Enterprises ULC, operating as Harlequin Reader Service. For a complete summary of the information we collect, how we use this information and to whom it is disclosed, please visit our privacy notice located at corporate.harlequin.com/privacy-notice. From time to time we may also exchange your personal information with reputable third parties. If you wish to opt out of this sharing of your personal information, please visit readerservice.com/consumerschoice or call 1-800-873-8635. **Notice to California Residents**—Under California law, you have specific rights to control and access your data. For more information on these rights and how to exercise them, visit corporate.harlequin.com/california-privacy.

LIRLIS23

HARLEQUIN
PLUS

Try the best multimedia subscription service for romance readers like you!

Read, Watch and Play.

Experience the easiest way to get the romance content you crave.

Start your **FREE TRIAL** at
<u>www.harlequinplus.com/freetrial</u>.